The phone rang again.

Aaron Miller cursed under his breath. Running a hand over his weary features, he closed his eyes and found himself wishing that he could just pick up the phone, could just talk to her and tell her what was going on.

He couldn't do that.

It would be her death sentence.

"This is Aaron," he heard the answering machine say, "and I can't take your call right now, but if you'll leave a message, I promise that I'll get back to you as soon as I can. Thanks."

BEEP.

There was a pause, and then came the voice that he hated to hear, the voice that tore him open.

"Daddy, it's Stephanie," came the frightened voice, and it ripped into him. "I've been calling you and calling you. Please, call me back. I don't know why you're not returning my calls. If I've done something to make you upset, just call me so that we can talk it out. You know that I hate this, Daddy. Please, call me."

He went towards the phone, but the sound of her hanging up paused him in his tracks.

Miller went over to the couch and collapsed on it.

There had to be a way that he could get out of this. He knew that, but no matter how hard he tried, he couldn't find a way out of the situation.

If he told anyone, the consequences would be disastrous.

His hands were tied.

A few moments later, the phone rang again, and he buried his head in his hands.

Finally, he answered it.

"Hello, Aaron," came the voice he had come to hate.

"What do you want?" he asked, his voice barely audible. "Why won't you leave me alone?"

"Aaron, I just need for you to do one more little favor for me, and then, I'm out of your life forever."

Miller shook his head. "You're lying."

"Come on now – let's not be stupid here. You know what will happen if you don't do as I ask. Do me this one last favor, and that will be the end of it. I promise."

"What do you want from me now?"

There was a pause.

"Meet me at the villa and I'll explain everything."

"I want your word that – " Miller began, but the caller had already hung up.

CHAPTER ONE

Professor James Hale studied his reflection in the mirror, adjusting his tie. It still didn't quite look right, but it would have to do. After all, he was a history professor, and not a fashion model.

He took a deep breath and stared at himself.

"The storming of the Bastille," he said, his voice strong, projecting outwards, "marked a new chapter in the history of France. It signaled the end of the monarchy and the beginning of a republican nation. For too long, those who had bore the weight of a ruthless tyranny had endured endless suffering, until they could no longer take it.

"For the citizens of France, the storming of the Bastille symbolized liberty and democracy, as well as an unspoken promise that never again will people stand idly by and allow themselves to be made slaves."

At that moment, his attention was drawn to the television that was on in the background.

He turned to look at the news anchor – a typical mannequin with perfect hair, perfect smile, and no understanding as to what it meant to be an actual journalist.

"The President is moving for the Upper Chamber of Parliament to pass a bill that France is to opt out of the Eurodollar. Here is a report of the Parliamentary debate…"

Hale's eyes narrowed.

What was going on?

The camera focused on the President of France, aristocratic and elegant, standing behind a lectern, looking out at the assembly.

If he was nervous, he didn't show it. Then again, as a trained politician, he was accustomed to always appearing to be in control, even when things were obviously going awry.

"…a single interest rate for EU member nations will

undermine stability. When rates are too low, there will be inflation – and when rates are too high, there will be recession and unemployment."

Movement from the right side of the chamber drew his attention, and he watched as a heavyset man in his late forties rose, his dark eyes bright with energy.

Senator Pierce Byron – naturally.

Where there were cameras around, it was a sure bet that Senator Byron would not be far behind.

"Mr. President, what about the benefits of the Eurodollar? Isn't it time that we introduced a universal currency that meets the demands of trade? A single monetary standard has usually followed the expansion of political power. The benefits of the Eurodollar far outweigh any negatives."

"We should not lose sight of the fact that there are many severe economic problems attached. The economy is this nation's lifeblood. We can't afford to be plunged into poverty. Should that happen, development and education and national defense will grind to a halt. Opting out of the Eurodollar is a definite move in the right direction."

The camera cut back to the news anchor.

"The Upper Chamber took a vote on the bill and received a majority vote of support for passage. The President will now forward the bill to the Lower Chamber of the National Assembly to motion for passage."

Hale picked up the remote and turned off the television.

"God, politicians must love the sound of their own voice, that's for sure. Nothing ever changes for them. It's all one tremendous game."

Shaking his head in disgust, he picked up his notecards, looked at his reflection one more time, and headed out the door.

"Time to knock 'em dead," he muttered.

***

Looking out over the sea of faces watching him intently, Hale felt that familiar thrill as he realized that he had them in the palm of his hand.

It was times like this that he truly loved being a professor, sharing his knowledge with his students and friends.

"Now, picture if you will, that day two hundred years ago – when the people of France rose up as one entity and stormed the prison that was meant for the aristocrats but was nothing more than a symbol of feudalism.

"No longer would these people stand idly by and tolerate King Louis XVI's heavy and disgustingly unfair tax regime.   The storming of the Bastille marked a new chapter in the history of France.   This was the end of monarchy and the beginning of a republican nation.

"For the citizens of France, the storming of the Bastille symbolizes liberty and democracy and the struggle to throw off the chains of oppression.   A people that had once been looked upon as pathetic and nothing more than objects of derision strode into history and succeeded in toppling a regime that was corrupt and unhealthy.

"History is a mirror that allows us to see ourselves through our pasts and to learn lessons from what we see, helping us to keep from going down roads that have led others to ruin.   History shows us the mistakes of others so that we can keep from making them, and so that the world that we live in can grow and prosper and become better than any of us could dream.

"And on that note, let me wind down and let all of you get out of here.   Thanks for coming."

He was met with thunderous applause.

For a moment, though, his attention was drawn to a figure near by back door of the auditorium.   Hale couldn't make out the man's features – if it was a man – but he noticed the man just stood there while everyone else stood and clapped.

Oh, well, he thought, *I guess I can't please everyone.*

***

Hale was putting up his papers when an incredibly attractive redhead came over to him, standing directly in front of him.

Looking into the emerald eyes of Stephanie Miller, he gave her a broad smile and said, "You almost looked like you were paying attention a couple of times, Steph. I'm impressed."

She laughed. "What can I say? I had a couple of extra coffees on the way here and they helped keep me awake."

Stephanie Miller, in addition to being the daughter of his best friend, was also Hale's best student and the one that he saw most likely to follow in his footsteps when it came to history.

He put the last of his papers into his briefcase and said, "Well, I'm certainly looking forward to your paper on Tuesday. I'm sure that it'll be every bit as entertaining as you found my lecture tonight."

She stopped smiling and Hale instantly sensed a change in the mood. "Professor Hale, is there any way that I can get an extension on the paper?"

Hale sighed. "Steph, you know that you're my favorite student and you know that your dad's my best friend. The problem is that all the other students know that, too, and if I give you any leeway, I'll have a lot of angry students hounding me. What seems to be the problem?"

"I just need a little more time, that's all," she said, and she wouldn't meet his eyes.

Hale frowned. "What's going on?" he asked.

She finally met his gaze, and he was astonished to see tears in her eyes. "It's my father."

"Aaron? What's wrong? Is he sick?"

"That's just it. I don't know."

Hale frowned. "I'm afraid that I'm not following you."

"I've been trying to reach my father for days, but he's not returning any of my calls. He's never done anything like this before and I don't like it."

"Well, I'll admit that doesn't sound like your father. He's about the most responsible man I know."

"I just wish I knew what was going on."

"What's he been working on?"

Stephanie shook her head. "I'm not sure. He didn't tell me much about it – but I know that it dealt with having to verify a Rembrandt."

"It's been years since Aaron's done a verification. Which painting was being examined?"

"I think it was 'Musical Allegory.'"

Hale bit his lower lip, trying to recall where he had recently heard that particular Rembrandt mentioned.

After a moment, he nodded. "There was a bit on CNN last month on that painting. Edgard Cheever bought it, I think."

She nodded. "I'm sure you're right."

Hale sighed. "As always, the rich manage to get their hands on the priceless treasures of the world, and the rest of the world has to stand in line in museums that are falling apart just to get a glimpse of them."

Stephanie gave him a long look. "I know that I really don't have the right to ask this of you, but I was hoping that you might – " she began, then shook her head. "No. Never mind."

He gave her a warm smile and held up a hand. "You want me to see if I can find out anything?"

"I know that this isn't your responsibility, but – "

Hale put a hand on her shoulder. "Aaron's always been a terrific friend and I'd be a real jerk if I didn't help him out when he needed me."

"It might be nothing," she said.

"True – but we're not going to find that out until we check it out, right?   So, let's go and see if we can't find out if Cheever knows anything."

Stephanie frowned. "Right now?"

"No sense in wasting time, is there?   No time like the present."

CHAPTER TWO

As they drove to Cheever's villa, Hale tried to think of anywhere that his old friend might be hiding, but he drew a complete blank.

He found it difficult to keep from looking at Stephanie. She was beautiful and bright and everything that a man would look for in a woman – and she was also the daughter of his best friend, which meant that he couldn't afford to think of her that way.

He forced his thoughts back to the situation. "No matter how I come at it," he told Stephanie, "I can't imagine where your father is."

"I know that Dad can get obsessed when he's on the track of something," she said, "but he's never just dropped out of sight for this long – not when he's somewhere civilized. I know there are times when he's been in some Third World country that didn't have any electrical power, but the moment that he was able to reach me, he called."

Hale frowned. "If it were anyone other than Cheever, I don't think I'd be nearly this worried," he said. "But Cheever's reputation as a snake is world-renowned. In fact, I think I just read where the man is facing yet another series of police probes linking him to various black market activities."

Stephanie shook her head. "I'm having a hard time believing that my father would even work for a man like Cheever."

Hale chuckled. "Actually, that's the part that I understand."

She gave him a curious look. "Mind explaining that to me?"

"Simple – your father is a genuine art lover. For the chance to actually spend time with a genuine Rembrandt, your father would put up with a great deal."

"That's true."

Hale pulled into the driveway of a huge villa, pausing before a large set of wrought-iron gates. There was a callbox with a red button on it.

Hale pressed the button. "Hello?"

After a few moments, a female voice, distorted by the speakers, said, "Hello. Can I help you?"

"I'm James Hale and with me is Stephanie Miller. We'd like a few minutes of Mr. Cheever's time."

There was a pause.

"Do you have an appointment?"

"No. This is something that just came up."

"I'm sorry, but Mr. Cheever doesn't see anyone without an appointment."

Hale felt a sharp stab of irritation. "Tell you what — please tell Mr. Cheever he can either speak with us or he can speak with the police. The choice is his."

"Please wait one moment."

There was a pause and Stephanie gave Hale a surprised look. "I didn't expect something like that out of you."

"If there's one thing that I hate, it's when some of these rich idiots think that their time is more valuable than someone else's. If anything, they have a lot more leisure time than most people."

"Mr. Cheever will see you for a few minutes," came the woman's voice, and the gates slowly swung inwards.

***

Hale drove up the long, winding drive towards the massive villa.

Actually, calling it a "villa" would be an understatement. It was more along the lines of a modern-day mansion, albeit one decorated with the trappings of classical architecture.

Emerging from the car, Hale stood there, taking in the large marble columns, the hand-laid mosaic tiles leading into the house.

The massive front door opened, and a tall, elegant butler stood there, regarding them with cool detachment.

"If you would please follow me," the man said, turning around, walking away.

Hale and Stephanie followed.

The interior of the mansion was mind-boggling. Hale couldn't even begin to think of the kind of money that it must have taken to create a home like this. No, it wasn't even really a home. If anything, it was more like a museum.

Wonder if they've got a gift shop, he thought.

As they were led down several corridors, Hale spotted two Picassos and three Van Goghs adorning the walls, and he slowly let out a whistle. "I haven't seen specimens like this since I worked as a curator at the Louvre for a summer," he whispered.

Stephanie just looked at her surroundings in astonishment.

They were finally led to a large drawing room, where they found Edgard Cheever sitting behind a massive hard-carved oak desk.

Cheever was fit, in his late-fifties, with penetrating dark eyes and a slightly sardonic smile on his lips.

He rose from behind the desk and went over to Hale, hand extended. "Professor Hale. It is, indeed, an honor to meet you."

Hale shook Cheever's hand, but there was no warmth in the greeting.

"You know who I am," Hale commented.

Cheever chuckled. "Indeed, I do. I make it a point of knowing everyone that I need to know," he said, and then turned his attention to Stephanie, who regarded him with cool detachment. "I don't believe I've had the pleasure," he said, with a broad smile.

"This is Stephanie Miller," Hale said.

Cheever gave an elegant little bow. "My pleasure," he said, then went over to his desk, sitting down. "Now, why don't you have a seat and tell me what I can do for you."

Hale sat down and regarded Cheever in silence for a few moments.

The businessman returned his stare with calm amusement. Finally, he said, "Professor, I believe you mentioned something about the police earlier. Would you care to explain?"

"I'd like to talk to you about Rembrandt's 'Musical Allegory.'"

Cheever nodded. "It's quite an impressive painting, isn't it? I didn't realize that you were such an art lover, Professor."

"Actually, I'm here because of my friendship with Aaron Miller."

"Ah, now it's beginning to make sense. You're here because you want to make sure that your friend is going to get paid for the work he did for me."

Hale frowned. "Excuse me?"

"That's why you're here, isn't it? It seems that my assistant forgot to pay Professor Miller for his excellent work in verifying my Rembrandt. Naturally, I'll make sure that I give you a check before you leave."

Hale shook his head. "No. That's not why we're here."

"It isn't? What can I do for you, then?"

"Professor Miller is missing. I'm helping his daughter track him down."

Cheever looked surprised. "Missing? That hardly seems like the professor.   Still, if he's anything like some of the other academics that I've dealt with, he might have simply gotten excited about some new project and lost track of time."

Stephanie shook her head. "That's not the way my father is – not when it comes to keeping in touch with me."

"Mr. Cheever, why did you have Aaron verify the Rembrandt? It was verified prior to your purchasing it at auction, wasn't it?"

Cheever nodded. "Indeed, it was. However, the new buyer wanted to make sure that it had flawless credentials, and he insisted upon another verification."

That caught Hale by surprise. He hadn't realized that Cheever had sold the Rembrandt to someone else.   "You sold the Rembrandt?"

Cheever chuckled. "Indeed, I did.   I had it in my possession for less than a week when someone came along and wanted to purchase it from me. Naturally, I agreed."

"Who was the buyer?"

Cheever gave Hale a long look. "Naturally, I can count on your complete confidence?"

"Of course."

"I sold it to Peter Ackerman."

"Of Ackerman Oil?"

"Naturally."

Hale thought about that and nodded. It made sense. Ackerman was a definite art collector, and having a genuine Rembrandt would be very appealing.

Hale frowned. "Naturally, Mr. Ackerman will verify what you've told us?"

Cheever gave Hale a cold look. "Yes, he would – if you were to speak with him, but I'd rather that you didn't do that."

"I need to check all avenues, I'm afraid."

Cheever narrowed his eyes. "Professor Hale, I feel that I've been quite gracious in dealing with you. Now, however, I'm afraid that you've grown tiresome. If I were you, I'd walk away from this right now."

Hale shook his head. "I can't do that."

"Well, in that case, I really recommend that you keep both myself and Mr. Ackerman out of this. If you don't, I'm afraid that I might have to bring the authorities into this."

Hale rose, staring intently at Cheever. "You do what you have to do, Mr. Cheever – and I'll do the same."

***

Outside Cheever's house, Hale and Stephanie stood by the car.

Hale's attention was on the closed front door, and he said, in a soft voice, "I don't know about you, but my gut told me that Cheever was definitely trying to put something over on us."

Hale noticed that one of the curtains nearby was off to one side, and although he couldn't be sure, he imagined that he saw someone standing there, looking out at them.

Stephanie nodded. "I got the exact same feeling."

"I couldn't help but notice when I mentioned going to see Ackerman that he got slightly upset. That tells me that something's going on there that we need to look into."

She gave him a worried look. "He said that he was going to call the police on you if you caused problems. Do you think he's serious?"

Hale chuckled. "Definitely not. Men like Cheever do not use the authorities unless it's absolutely necessary. They prefer to always fly below the radar."

"What do you think's going on?"

Hale thought about it for a few minutes. "To be honest, I'm not sure. My gut tells me that Cheever is definitely involved in whatever your father is mixed up in."

"So, what's next?"

"I think we need to talk to Ackerman and find out if he has any idea where your father might be."

"I've got a feeling that Cheever's not going to like us stirring things up."

Hale shrugged. "Frankly, I couldn't care less – the only thing that matters to me is finding your father."

***

CHAPTER THREE

Heading down the highway at speeds approaching somewhat dangerous, Hale drove towards the address that one of his students had provided for Peter Ackerman. The young man had a father who worked in the Department of Transportation, and he'd located Ackerman's vehicle license information.

"Actually, Professor, there are two addresses listed. Do you want both of them?" Eddie Doyle had asked.

Hale had taken both addresses, and now he was heading towards the first of them.

Stephanie cleared her throat, and Hale shot a quick glance at her.

"What's wrong?" he asked.

She gave him a searching look. "I want to ask you something, and I want you to tell me the truth."

Hale's stomach churned, and he took a deep breath. He'd wondered when this would be coming. "What's that?" he asked.

"Do you think that my father's all right?"

Hale stared straight ahead, wondering how best to answer her. On the one hand, he believed in being honest whenever possible, but right now, he knew that Stephanie did not need honesty.

She needed hope.

"Yes," he lied, hating himself for doing so, "I think that your father is fine."

In less than half an hour, Hale would find himself regretting those words.

***

Hale and Stephanie stood in front of the large, wrought-iron gates, and Hale pressed the button for the third time.

No response.

"I guess this is the part where we turn around and come up with another approach?"

Hale shook his head. "Not necessarily."

"What do you have planned?"

He looked up at the gates, and Stephanie shook her head.

"Don't be ridiculous. There's no way that – "

Before she could finish, Hale had begun to climb the gates. He did a fairly impressive job of climbing over, right until the leg of his pants got caught on one of the wrought-iron spikes.

Stephanie turned away, trying to hide her amusement.

"Instead of taking such a perverse delight in my making a fool of myself, why don't you give me a hand?"

Stephanie giggled, and climbed up enough to help him remove his pants from the gate.

Hale scaled down on the other side of the gate. "I'll be right back.   Wait here."

"As opposed to waiting where?" she asked, but he was already heading down the path that led to the house.

Hale moved quickly down the path, doing his best to maintain a low profile and also to keep his eyes open for anything suspicious.

When he reached the front door and saw that it was ajar, a cold feeling went through him.

"Not good," he muttered, and climbed the steps leading to the house.

When he reached the door, he pushed it open wider, and called out, "Hello?   Is anyone here?"

There was no answer.

He stood there for a long moment, and knew that the smart thing to do would be to call the authorities. But, if he did that and Aaron were inside in need of help, he'd never forgive himself.

Hale entered the house.

Moving carefully forward, he found himself wishing that he had some kind of weapon. Whenever someone walked into an unlocked house in the movies, there was never anything good to be found inside.

Everything about the interior furnishings screamed wealth and excess, but he paid them little mind, more interested in finding out what was going on.

When he reached the living room, he felt his world spin around.

There was a body, lying face down, in a pool of blood – and even before he turned it over, he knew that he'd found his missing friend.

In that moment, he also knew that he was going to find who had done this and he was going to make sure that they paid for their crime.

He reached for his cell phone, and his attention was caught by something next to the body.

It was a playing card.

The King of Spades.

Next to the card was a piece of paper that had a cryptic message typed on it:

Jesse The roots The Shepherd Father of all greatness.

He set the paper and the card down on the floor, and punched a number into the cell phone. "Something tells me that I just stepped into a whole lot of messy," he muttered, waiting for the police to pick up the phone.

***

Kneeling beside Medical Examiner Sidney Larway, Chief Inspector Frankie Darley looked down at the body and shook his head.

Over twenty years working cases like this, and he never got used to death. For some police officers, it just became a job – a way of collecting a paycheck. For Darley, it was always about justice – about making sure that those who committed crimes paid.

Larway rubbed the top of his balding head and sighed. "If you're looking for a time of death, about the only thing that I can give you is it's between twenty-four and forty-eight hours. I can't do better than that."

Darley nodded. "That's fine. It's something, at least."

"Cause of death?"

"Stab wound, looks like."

"Murder?" Darley asked and Larway chuckled.

"Unless the victim managed to stab himself and hide the weapon, I'm going to have to do with murder."

Darley grinned, relishing the easy camaraderie he'd developed through the years with the M.E.

The two men rose and Darley said, "Let's go and meet the guy who called this in."

CHAPTER FOUR

Hale sat at the kitchen table, arm around a sobbing Stephanie.

He was still having problems believing that his friend was dead. It made absolutely no sense. Who in the world would have wanted to kill Aaron? The man didn't have an enemy in the world.

Well, he had at least one enemy, he thought.

Looking over in the doorway, he saw a tall, muscular figure watching him intently. The man had penetrating eyes and Hale instantly recognized him as a police officer.

He came over and looked down at Hale. "Professor Hale?"

"Yes."

"I'm Chief Inspector Darley."

The two men shook hands, and Darley turned to Stephanie. "I'm sorry for your loss, Ms. Miller."

Stephanie nodded and turned to Hale. "I think I want to get some fresh air."

"That's a good idea."

The two men waited for her to leave, and once she was gone, Darley said, "You were the one who found the body, am I correct?"

Hale nodded. "Yeah. I called it in immediately."

"What was your relationship with the deceased?"

"He was a close friend."

"And what is your relationship to Peter Ackerman?"

Hale shook his head. "I've never met the man."

Darley regarded him with raised eyebrows. "You've never met the man – and yet, you climbed his gate, trespassed upon his property, and entered his home without an invitation. I find that rather curious, Professor Hale."

Hale stared into Darley's eyes and saw that he was

definitely dealing with someone who was clever and sharp. "Stephanie came to me because she hadn't heard from her father. I did some investigating and discovered that he had been hired to verify a painting for Ackerman. When we arrived here, no one rang us in and I decided to scale the gate and see if someone was here and just didn't want to answer the intercom.

"Instead, I found Aaron – dead."

"Did you happen to notice the objects by the body?"

"Yes – and I picked them up, I'm afraid."

Darley gave him a long look. "Why would you do something like that?"

"At the time, I wasn't thinking. I saw my friend lying on the floor and I just reacted."

"Those are important pieces of evidence. You shouldn't have handled them."

"Yes, I realize that now," Hale said, somewhat testily.

"What did you think of the objects?"

"Well, I'm not sure. If I didn't know better, I'd say that you're dealing with someone who wants to play games with you."

"What makes you think that?"

"The playing card has to have something to do with games, I'd say. It was obviously left there as some kind of message."

Darley nodded. "Possibly. Then again, it might have something to do with your friend and whether or not he has a gambling problem."

Hale chuckled. "That's definitely out of the question. Aaron never believed in anything even remotely having to do with games of chance. He felt they were designed to take advantage of weak-willed people."

Darley pondered this. "If you're right – and, for the moment, let us assume you are – whoever did this wanted to taunt the police. That means they wouldn't have been the one to call it in. Instead, they'd like to stand on the sidelines, watching as we attempted to discover who they were. The kind of person who plays games like this never wants to be anywhere near the spotlight."

"So, where do we go from here?"

Darley raised an eyebrow. "'We?'"

Hale crossed his arms. "Look, Inspector, I know that you've got a job to do, and I definitely respect that. But, Aaron was my closest friend, and that means that I'm not about to just walk away from this. If I did that, I'd never be able to look at myself in the mirror again."

Darley stared at him for a long moment. "I certainly appreciate the sentiment, Professor Hale, but right now, we're in the middle of something that is probably best handled by professionals. You have my word that I'll do everything in my power to bring the person behind this to justice, but for now, the best thing that you can do is just let the professionals handle it."

Hale sighed. "I hate not being able to do anything."

"We will find your friend's murderer. You have my word on that."

***

Sitting at his desk back at the station, Darley examined the playing card and the note that had been left at the scene and shook his head.

He hated dealing with cases like this. When it came to crimes, Darley liked things simple and straightforward – not playing games with some psycho who needed to see if they were smarter than the police. In the end, they always wound up getting caught, but usually not before the press got hold of the situation and managed to blow things out of proportion.

Darley hated having to deal with the press. Reporters accomplished nothing more than making a cop's job more difficult. If they came across any kind of clue that might be newsworthy, they didn't have any problem with going public with it – and that made the criminals much more likely to go ahead to either change their strategies or else to leave town.

At that moment, Sergeant Garen Fasset came over, and sat down next to the desk.

Fasset was young, handsome, and one of the up-and-comers that were showing up so often in the police force these days. He was ambitious and he was sharp – a volatile combination, at times.

"Print results?" Darley asked.

"The only ones we got were from Hale."

Darley nodded.

"That's pretty much what I was expecting."

Fasset put his hands behind his head, relaxing. "You're sure that Hale isn't involved with this?"

"For the moment, I'm sure – but that is subject to change. I've been around enough criminals to know when someone is lying to me and when they're being honest, and Hale was not lying to me. That doesn't mean that he's not involved in some other way, though. Only time will tell."

"So, what do we do?"

Darley sipped his coffee. "We go out on a fishing expedition. I want to put the word out on the street that we want any information about Aaron Miller or James Hale."

"What about it just being a psycho playing games?"

Darley shook his head. "No. It's not a psycho."

"What makes you so sure?"

"There are a lot of rich people involved. When it comes

to the wealthy, there's usually always more going on than meets the eye."

Fasset nodded. "You might be right. What about Ackerman?"

Darley shook his head.

"Forget it. He's been in Germany for the past two days. He's due back in town tomorrow."

"Let's say that we want to take Hale at face value. If he's telling the truth, there's someone else that we might want to take a look at."

Darley sighed.

"I know – Edgard Cheever."

"You don't sound enthusiastic."

"I tend to get that way when I have to question a man who can have my job with one single phone call."

"That's why you get paid the big bucks," Fasset said.

Darley stared at him. "I don't know where you get your information from, but if I'm getting the big bucks, I'd hate to see what the little bucks look like."

"That would be my salary," Fasset commented.

"In that case, you can come with me to question Cheever. That way, if he decides to get both of us fired, it won't hurt you to lose those little bucks you get paid."

CHAPTER FIVE

Fasset and Darley sat in Edgard Cheever's living room, both of them clearly uncomfortable, as the multi-millionaire regarded them with a cold gaze.

Standing over them, he said, "I'm afraid that you caught me at a bad time, gentlemen. I'm in the middle of some very sensitive business negotiations. What is it that you need from me?"

"Professor Aaron Miller was murdered," Darley said.

"I see."

"You don't seem very upset."

Cheever chuckled. "Inspector, I hired the man to authenticate a painting for me. Period. Since I didn't know him personally, why on earth would I pretend to care whether or not he lived or died?"

"It's just that – "

Cheever shook his head, glancing at his watch. "Gentlemen, as much as I'd like to help you, I'm on a very tight schedule here. If I think of anything that can help you, I'll get in touch with you."

And with that, he left the room.

***

Driving away from Cheever's estate, Darley shook his head. Fasset glanced over at him as he drove, and said,

"So, what are you thinking about Cheever?"

Darley snorted. "I'm thinking that he's definitely not crossed off my list yet."

"Why's that?"

"You saw how he treated us. The man was definitely hiding something."

Fasset chuckled. "I think you're giving him too much credit. I've been around enough rich people to know that they all act like that. Guys like us aren't important enough for them to hide anything from."

"What really pisses me off," Darley said, tapping lightly on the brakes as the car in front of them began to slow down, "is that I wind up having to tiptoe around him so that he doesn't get pissed off at me and make a phone call."

Fasset nodded. "Yeah, I know. That's the thing about big money – it gets to do things that nobody else does. The rich are different, that's for sure."

Darley's phone rang and he took it from his pocket. "Hello?...Yes...Fine. We'll be right there."

Putting the phone away, he glanced over at Fasset. "Ackerman's back in town. Let's go and see what he knows."

**

Darley looked around the drawing room where he and Fasset waited, knowing that there was more money spent in that one space than he earned in a year. Artwork that he didn't recognize but suspected were quite well-known adorned the walls, and the built-in bookshelves contained leather-bound volumes that were probably first editions and priceless.

A middle-aged man losing his hair entered the room, dressed in what Darley identified as an Armani suit, came into the room.

Darley and Fasset turned to him, and he looked at them as if he could see right through them.

"I was told that you're with the police?" Ackerman asked.

The two men took out their badges and flashed them.

Ackerman nodded. "What is it that I can do for you?"

"We're here about Professor Aaron Miller," Darley said.

Ackerman raised his eyebrows.

"Has he done something wrong?"

"What is your connection with Professor Miller?"

"I hired him to verify a painting that I wished to purchase."

"Were you aware that he was murdered?"

Ackerman's eyes widened.

"What?   When did this happen?"

"It probably took place about three days ago."

"Do you know who killed him?"

"No.   In fact, we were hoping that you might be able to help us."

Ackerman gave him a long look. "What makes you think that?"

"Do you have anything that we might be able to use?"

Ackerman frowned. "I might have some ideas, but right now, I wouldn't want to share them with you."

"Why is that?"

"There are some people involved who could be hurt by unsubstantiated rumors, as I'm sure you can understand. If I were to just put their names out there without finding out the truth, you can see how they might be damaged."

Darley shook his head. The last thing in the world he cared about right now was dealing with some rich person's reputation. "Do you understand that a murder has been committed? I'd think that would be an important factor in whatever problems you're having with telling us what you know."

"I'm sorry, Inspector."

Darley tried to keep his temper under control. It wasn't easy. "You realize that we can have you brought in for questioning," he said, his voice tight.

Ackerman gave him a cold look. "Yes, I realize that. And I'm sure that you realize that if you bring me in, I will have my attorney show up and make sure that I don't answer a single question. The way that I see it, Inspector, you can either wait for me to contact you, after I've done some digging on my own – or you can bring me in and know that you won't get anything out of me."

Darley took a deep breath. "Let's try something else, then – you hired Professor Miller to authenticate a painting that was being sold by Edgard Cheever."

"Yes."

"Did you suspect it wasn't genuine?"

Ackerman shook his head. "On the contrary – I was actually certain that it was an original, but since I'm not an art expert, I thought it wise to hire someone who actually might know for certain. In the business world, it's always best to know what one's weaknesses are so that they can be offset by surrounding yourself with people who have strengths in those areas."

"Was it genuine?"

Ackerman nodded. "It was."

"I'd love to see the painting," Darley said.

Disgust etched itself into the millionaire's face. "You and me both, Inspector. The painting was entrusted to my assistant, since I had a business meeting in Germany that I could not miss. I've been trying to reach my assistant since we landed, without success."

The police inspector regarded Ackerman with surprise. "You left a priceless painting with your assistant?"

Ackerman nodded. "The man has been with me for over ten years. He's as close to family as anyone around me."

Darley took out his notepad. "Can I get a name from you?"

"Hugh Jetter."

"Just so I can get this time line straight in my head –

was it Hugh Jetter who was with Professor Miller when the painting was being authenticated?"

"Yes."

"Well, this is certainly an interesting yarn that you're spinning here.   I wonder if you realize – "

"I am not 'spinning' anything, Inspector.   I'm telling you what happened."

Darley shrugged. "We'll see about that."

Ackerman stared at him. "Are you making any accusations, Inspector?   If you are, you should be aware that your Commissioner and I are good friends, and you might find yourself in a bind, should your comments turn out not to hold water."

Darley held up a hand in mock surrender. "Please – don't misunderstand me, Mr. Ackerman.   I was just thinking out loud, that's all."

Ackerman gives him a skeptical look.

CHAPTER SIX

Darley, behind the wheel, turned his attention to Fasset, who was looking out the window, lost in thought.

"What do you think?" Darley asked.

Fasset turned to him. "I was wondering the same thing. How did he seem to you?"

Darley shook his head. "I'm not sure. He was definitely acting suspicious, but without anything solid, there isn't anything that we can do, that's for sure. I'm sure he's got his lawyer on speed dial and the minute that we tried to bring him in, he'd close up tighter than a clam, and we wouldn't get anything out of him."

Fasset nodded. "I'm sure you're right. In fact, it seemed like he was pushing you to come right out and accuse him so that he'd have an excuse not to cooperate with us."

"Well, about the only thing that we can do right now is check out Hugh Jetter and find out what his story is."

***

Holding the King of Spades in his hand, Hale paced around his living room, speaking loud enough so that the voice recorder on the coffee table could pick up his words.

There were answers to be found, he knew, but he didn't if he would be able to figure out just what those answers were.

Taking out a piece of paper, he read aloud the words he'd copied from the poem next to the body:

"Jesse The roots The Shepherd Father of all greatness."

Pacing some more, he sat down on the couch, and picked up the tape recorder, bringing it close to his mouth. "We have the King of Spades and we have a poem – and a badly written poem, at that. Right now, I don't mind saying that I don't have the slightest idea where this is going. I hope that the police have a better handle on this than I do."

He set the tape recorder down, then picked up the bottle

of wine.

Holding it aloft, he declared, as if he were back on the stage in his college years, "You sing to me, like a siren, from the shore – and I, ever faithful, come to thee."

And with that, Hale uncorked the wine, poured it into a glass, and downed it quickly.

***

The ringing of the cell phone snapped Hale awake, and through bleary eyes, he spotted his phone on the coffee table – right next to the empty bottle of wine.

"Hello?"

There was a pause, and then, a familiar voice came screaming into his ears.

Hale, wincing, moved the phone away.

"James!   How the hell are you?"

"Lionel Rousseau!   Damn, it's been too long!" Hale said, lowering his voice as the throbbing in his head which had suddenly come on decided to kick things up a notch.

"Guess where I am?"

"Last I heard, you were in Jerusalem on one of your digs," Hale said.

"I'm in France. I just landed."

"Terrific. We'll have to get together."

There was a pause.

"Yes, we definitely will. James, I've come back with something that is of tremendous historical significance."

Hale sighed. "You've got the life.   You actually are out there, living the dream, and I'm stuck lecturing to rich kids and going home to frozen dinners. So, what did you discover this time?"

"Well, one thing that I discovered is that people think the grass is actually greener in the desert."

"So, how about filling me in on what you've got going

on?"

There was another pause.

"This isn't something that can be revealed over the phone. It's something that you'll have to see in person."

Hale shook his head "Not tonight. Besides, you always make me come to you."

"Have you ever been disappointed?"

Hale chuckled. "No."

"Come to my place – and prepare to be amazed."

CHAPTER SEVEN

Hale pulled up in front of Rouseeau's house and sat in the car for a moment.

He wasn't the sort of man who was overly paranoid, but with the recent events taking place, he couldn't help but feel that someone as playing with him – and that meant that he wasn't about to trust anyone.

He and Lionel Rouseeau went way back – to their college days. Even back then, Lionel had led a charmed life. Things came easily to him – girls, grades, gold. Hale, on the other hand, had always had to struggle, and while some people might have said that the struggle was good for the soul, there were times when Hale wished that his life were less of a struggle.

<u>Like right now,</u> he thought, opening the car door. <u>The last thing in the world I need is to get mixed up in a mess like this.</u>

Hale went up the steps to Rouseeau's house, and before he knocked, he saw that the door was slightly ajar.

He stared at it, and his gut tightened.

"There is no way this is going to turn out good," he muttered, and pushed the door open.

The smart thing, he knew, would be to stay right where he was, call the police, and let them handle it.

Hale entered the house.

Moving cautiously through the immaculate and tastefully furnished home, Hale saw a light at the end of a hallway coming from what looked like the study.

"Hello? Lionel?"

Silence.

Once again, Hale heard a little voice inside of him tell him to take out his phone and make a call, but he continued forward.

Standing outside the study, Hale took a deep breath and went inside.

At first, he didn't see anything out of the ordinary, and he was about to turn around when he saw something sticking out from the side of the couch.

Moving closer, he saw it was a shoe – and it was attached to a leg.

Hale saw Claire Pierpont's lifeless body on the carpet.

Chest covered in blood, her sightless eyes were wide and unfocused, and Hale found it hard to breathe. His heart was racing, and a wave of dizziness washed over him.

"This is crazy," he muttered. "Why the hell am I the one finding all the damned bodies around here?"

That's when he saw it.

A playing card beside the body.

Hale knew that touching it would be totally insane – but he needed to find out what the hell it was.

He picked it up and turned it over.

The King of Diamonds.

"Okay," he said, "that's two kings and two bodies. Obviously, someone's playing a sick game here and I need to get the hell out of it right now."

He took out his cell phone and dialed the number that Inspector Darley had given him.

He didn't look forward to the chewing out that he knew was coming.

***

Darley and Fasset knelt beside the body, and exchanged looks.

"What do you think?" Fasset asked.

"Well, I'm not expert, but I'm thinking that she was murdered."

"No – I mean, what do you think about Hale being at

the scene of two murders now? He's beginning to look really good as a suspect."

Darley shook his head. "I don't buy it. Whoever is doing this is playing games, and Hale wouldn't be that kind of person. Now, if you ask me, he's probably the kind of guy who could commit an untraceable murder, if he put his mind to it. But, he's definitely not into playing games."

Fasset frowned. "Unless he's really an awesome game player – and it would give him a tremendous charge to be jerking us around like this."

Darley glanced around at the police technicians going over the crime scene, and he spotted Hale off to the side.

He stood and went over to him.

Hale shook his head. "I can't believe this," he said. "This is absolutely insane."

Darley chuckled. "Funny – my partner is having a hard time believing this, as well. In fact, he's looking at you as our prime suspect."

"Can't say that I blame him. If I didn't know that I had nothing to do with this, I'd be looking at myself, too."

"What do you suggest?"

Hale shook his head. "I don't have a clue. I mean, you've got two murders on your hands, and no suspects, right? The press is going to have a field day with this. You need to get to the bottom of this."

Darley narrowed his eyes. "Professor, I can assure you that I intend to get to the bottom of this. Make no mistake – I am going to find the killer."

Hale held up a hand. "Whoa – hold on a minute. I didn't mean that to come out the way it did. I know that you're doing everything that you can, Inspector."

Darley slowly nodded. "Right now, I think that both of us have a lot on our minds, and we should probably concentrate on finding the killer. First, however, there are some things that I need to get out of the way – such as why you are here."

"I was here to see Lionel Rouseeau. He had something that he wanted to show me."

"Who is this Lionel Rouseeau?"

"He's an old friend – an archeologist."

"And where is he?"

Hale shook his head. "I don't know. I've been trying to reach him since I got here – without any success."

Darley made a note and said, "We'll try to find his locate and make sure that he's safe."

"What do you think's going on?"

Darley shrugged. "I'm not sure. It looks like it's the work of a serial killer – but I'm beginning to think that it's not."

"Why not?" Hale asked.

"I think there's something deliberate going on here, and it goes deeper than the two murders. I think something is going on behind the scenes."

"Such as?"

Darley shook his head. "I don't know. I think that when we figure that out, we'll find the person responsible for the two murders. In the meantime, I think that you'd better come downtown and fill out a report, answer some questions."

"Am I a suspect?"

Darley nodded. "Of course."

Hale sighed. "That's what I figured."

***

Barrie Beauchump maneuvered the Peugeot through the traffic, doing his best to ignore the incessant crunching coming from his passenger.

He glanced over at Daniel Cohen – and his bottomless

bag of pretzels.

At that moment, Cohen's cell phone rang and he put on the speakerphone.

"What's the situation?' Cohen asked.

"Hale's on the right track," the voice on the other end of the line said, deep and powerful. "He's linked the two murders, naturally, but he's going deeper than that."

Beauchump's gut tightened and he shot his passenger a worried look.

Damn it, he knew this was going to happen.

"Keep us in the loop," Cohen said. "Anything else we should know?"

"Not right now."

Cohen hung up and shoved another pretzel into his mouth.

Beauchump sighed. "I knew this was going to happen."

"Don't get bent out of shape."

"I knew from the first time I watched that damned professor teaching that he wasn't an idiot. He's the kind of guy who isn't going to fall for the obvious."

"You worry too much," Cohen said.

"Yeah, and you eat too many damned pretzels. You don't worry enough, Cohen. Maybe you don't mind going to prison, but I sure as hell don't want that."

"No one's going to prison."

He dialed a number and put the phone on speaker again.

One ring.

Two.

Three.

It was answered on the fourth ring.

"What is it?" came a soft, masculine voice.

"Something's come up."

"And that is -- ?"

"Hale might be getting close to the truth."

There was a long pause.

"How close?"

"I'm not sure."

"It's too soon for Hale to get to the truth."

"What do you want me to do?"

"I'm not sure yet. Let me look at our options and I'll get back to you."

Cohen hung up, and Beauchump shook his head.

"Nothing good is going to come of this. This is going to end badly."

CHAPTER EIGHT

Darley sat at his desk, tired and irritable.

He'd been through the photographs and the reports of both crime scenes, and he was still no closer to getting a handle on it than when he'd first started.

He looked across the desk at Fasset. "What do you think?"

"You know what I think – I think it stinks."

"You still like Hale for this, don't you?"

"It makes sense. The man was at the scene of both murders."

"He's not stupid, you know. He'd be an idiot to be so obvious."

Fasset gave him a long look. "Think about what happens if it turns out that he is the killer. The press would crucify us. They'd demand to know why we didn't go after him more thoroughly."

Darley sighed. "You're right about that."

"I think that we should get a search warrant. That way, we can cover all our bases."

"Do you really think that he's the killer?"

Fasset shrugged. "I think that we need to make sure of every avenue, my friend – because if you're wrong and he's responsible, you might as well just turn in your resignation and start looking for work as a security guard."

***

Looking at Stephanie sitting on his couch, softly crying, Hale desperately tried to think of something that he could say to help ease her pain. Unfortunately, there were no words to take this burden from her.

Hale sat beside her and put his arm around her. She buried her face in his shoulder, and he gently held her. He did his best not to think about how it felt to have her so close, how much he wanted to take her in his arms and tell her that he –

No, he wasn't going to go there.

"Your father was a great man," he said, softly, remembering the man who had been his mentor and his best friend. "He taught me everything that I know today, and instilled a love of history in me that's truly transformed me."

Stephanie wiped her eyes and turned to him. "I remember how happy he was when the two of you were working on your book on the French Revolution. He'd come home after being with you and talk about the discussions that you had. In some ways, I think that you were the son that he wanted."

Hale chuckled. "Hardly -- although we might have been brothers, I guess."

She shook her head. "When I first heard about it, I thought that there was some kind of mistake. I mean, we're talking about my father here. Who in the world would want to hurt him?"

Hale sighed. "I don't know. I keep coming back to that and I don't have a definite answer -- although I'm certain that the painting has something to do with it."

"Who do you think is behind it?"

"Right now, I don't have a clue. Are you sure that your father didn't say anything that might be able to lead us to the person responsible?"

Stephanie shook her head. "If he did, I'm not remembering it."

The doorbell rang.

"Well, you keep thinking on it. Maybe something will eventually come to you. I'll be right back."

He opened the door and found Darley and Fasset standing there.

Hale rolled his eyes. "Again? More questions?"

Darley handed him a document. "We have a search warrant, Professor Hale."

"You've got to be kidding me," Hale said, a slight edge to his voice. "You really want to go down that path?"

Darley looked apologetic. "Right now, we need to cover all our bases."

He sighed and stepped to one side. "Well, you might as well come in and get this over with. Needless to say, you're wasting your time."

Darley nodded. "I hope that you're right."

Hale went back into the living room, and answered Stephanie's questioning look. "It's the police," he explained. "They want to search the place."

She gave him a disbelieving look.

"Why?"

He shrugged. "I think that they're covering all their bases. That's how it was explained to me."

She glared at Fasset as he passed by the living room.

"This is absolutely incredible. The police should be out there, finding the person responsible for my father's death, and instead, they're wasting time by investigating you."

Hale sighed. "In a way, I can't really blame them. If it turns out that I did kill your father and they didn't investigate me thoroughly, they'd be crucified. The way I see it, if I let them cross me off the list of suspects, that'll be that much sooner they can go after the real killer."

Stephanie gave him a long look and laughed softly.

"You reminded me of my father just then. That's something that he would have said. The man was always able to keep his cool under all circumstances."

Hale and Stephanie waited as the police went room by room. As more and more time passed, it became obvious that both police officers were growing irritated and when Darley finally came into the living room, he looked disgusted.

"Nothing," he said.

Hale nodded. "I know. I'm sorry that you didn't find anything incriminating, inspector."

The detective gave him a long look. "I'm not upset over that, Hale. Hell, to be honest, I didn't really think I was going to find anything, but I had to make sure. I'm just sick of being in the middle of something that makes absolutely no sense."

Hale nodded. "I understand your frustration, and if it makes you feel any better, I'm doing everything possible from this end to try to help you out."

Darley stared at him. "You seem totally innocent, Hale, but I swear to God, if I find out that you're keeping something from me, I'll come down on your like a ton of bricks. Do we have an understanding?"

Hale nodded. "We definitely understand each other, Inspector. Now, there's just one thing that I want you to understand -- you'd better apply all your talents to finding Aaron's killer before I do."

Darley heard a coldness to Hale's voice that he would never have thought possible, and he nodded. "We'll do our best."

***

After the police departed, Stephanie and Hale spent a few minutes straightening up the apartment.

"You'd think that the least they could do after trashing the place would be to give us some garbage bags, at least," Hale said, putting some of the couch cushions back into place.

Stephanie glared at him. "I can't believe that they're still acting as if you're a suspect."

Hale sighed. "I've been around long enough to understand that part of what they're upset with is that there's all this pressure on them to get to the bottom of things, and right now, I'm about the only person they've got that they can go after."

"So, it doesn't matter that you're not my father's killer?"

Hale chuckled. "All that matters is that they make it look like they're hot on the trail of somebody that they can pin this on.   They both probably know that I'm not the killer, but they need to be out there doing something."

Stephanie gave Hale a long look. "Can I ask you something?"

"Sure."

"Do you think that we're ever going to find my father's killer?"

Hale's features hardened. "I know this much -- if they don't, I will.   For the killer's sake, let's hope they get to him before I do."

CHAPTER NINE

Hale opened the front door, and put his arm around Stephanie as he led her towards her car.

It was a beautiful night. The air was crisp without being cold, and the stars overhead were countless. For a moment, Stephanie and Hale just stared at the night sky.

Stephanie turned to Hale. "So, what are you going to do now?"

He sighed. "I don't know. That's what's killing me. If this were some kind of academic problem, I could just work at it until I cracked it. But, this is definitely out of my league. On the one hand, I want to be able to just walk away from this and leave it to the professionals -- but I'm beginning to think that the only chance we've got of finding your father's killer is for me to do it myself."

She shook her head. "We'll do it," she said.

Hale frowned.

Before he could respond to that, a pair of bright headlights suddenly came to life, blinding both of them.

There came the sound of an engine roaring, and without thinking, Hale threw himself on top of Stephanie, sending the two of them to the ground. His body lay on top of hers.

Hale heard screeching tires, and a moment later, the night was ripped apart by the sound of automatic gunfire.

He felt the air get displaced by a bullet that whizzed past his ear.

The headlights washed over the two of them as the vehicle sped away into the night.

For a long moment, Hale just lay on top of Stephanie, trying to get himself under control. Finally, he stood up, reaching down and grabbing her hand.

She threw herself into his arms and he held her,

stroking her hair, making comforting sounds.

"Let's get inside," he said, softly, "and let's get the police here."

***

Darley and Fasset stood in the living room, looking at a very agitated Hale. Off to the side, Stephanie sipped a glass of wine, a blanket wrapped around her. Despite the warmth of the apartment, she still shivered.

Hale looked at the two detectives. "I think the time's come for you to start earning your pay," he said, his voice harsh. "Instead of wasting time trying to decide whether or not I'm Miller's murderer, go on out there and find the real killer."

Fasset shook his head. "Just because someone may or may not have shot at you, Hale, doesn't mean that you're no longer a suspect."

Hale looked at Darley in astonishment. "Is he kidding me?   What the hell is he talking about?"

"Calm down, Hale.   We need to – "

"Don't tell me to calm down!   There's someone out there taking potshots at us. I think that gives me a little entitlement to being pissed off!"

"Did you get a look at who shot at you?" Darley asked.

"No," Hale said, shaking his head.   "They were parked across the street and they turned their lights on.   I couldn't see anything."

"So, you don't know what kind of car they were driving?"

Hale sighed. "No."

Fasset frowned. "So, someone shot at you -- but you don't know who.   They drove away in a car that you can't identify.   It seems like we're going to have a problem finding out who's behind this, Professor Hale.   Of course, it's kind of convenient that they missed you when they were shooting and that you can't actually point us in any direction."

"Are you saying that you think that I staged this?" Hale asked, astonished.

Fasset shrugged. "It's just one theory, of course."

Hale's face turned red and he went towards Fasset, but Darley stepped in between the two men. "The two of you had better come with us," he said. "Obviously, you can't stay here. Next time, they might not miss."

***

An hour later, Hale found himself and Stephanie sitting in Darley's office, staring at the two police officers at the other end of the room. Darley seemed perplexed, and Fasset continued to regard him with what looked like suspicion.

Darley picked up a pen, examined it for a few moments, then set it down.

He looked at Hale, and shook his head. "Your lives are in danger," he finally said.

Hale gave him an incredulous look. "That's all that you've got for me? You're telling me that our lives are in danger? No offense, inspector, but I picked up on that right around the time the bullets started flying past my head."

The police officer gave him a cold look. "Professor Hale, I understand that you're under a great deal of stress here, but I think it's important that you keep something in mind."

"What's that?"

"None of this would be happening if you hadn't decided to start your own investigation into the matter. If you had come to the authorities at the beginning, you would not be in this position."

Hale took a deep breath, even though he felt like screaming. "If I hadn't taken it on myself to do this investigation, inspector, I'd say there's a very good chance that nothing would be getting done."

Stephanie, aware that the argument was about to take a turn for the worse, put her hand on Hale's arm.

Fasset cleared his throat. When he had everyone's attention, he focused his gaze on Hale. "I think there's something that's really strange here," he said.

Hale knew that Fasset was addressing him. "What's that?"

"The M.O. has changed here. The killer -- or killers -- are taking a more direct approach. In the past, he or they seemed to want to take an 'up close and personal' operation. Now, they're coming at their victims with automatic weapons."

Hale nodded. "Right. That's how we know we're not dealing with the actual killer."

Fasset frowned. "Why would you say that? It's possible that the killer can use automatic weapons, you know."

"Oh, it's possible. But I don't think so. Personally, I think whoever shot at me and Stephanie had been hired by the actual killer. Take a look at the methods. The indoor killings are well thought-out and almost elegant, despite the violence involved. The shootings a couple of hours ago were hasty and sloppy. We're dealing with two different groups here."

Darley nodded. "I'm thinking that you're right, professor. In addition, I don't think that you were supposed to be killed tonight."

"A warning, then?" Hale guessed.

The police inspector nodded, his features grim. "I think so."

"So, where does that leave us?"

"Well, we're going to get you and Miss Hale into a safe house. That's the first order of business. Once we get you settled in, we'll try and work out our next step."

Hale turned to Stephanie, who regarded him with stunned disbelief.

"When is this going to end, James?"

He gave her a long look. "I wish I knew, Stephanie. I wish to God I knew."

***

When the police cruiser pulled up to the small house located in the middle of nowhere, Hale and Stephanie, seated in the back, exchanged looks.

Darley, driving, glanced in the rearview mirror and shrugged. "The way we see it, you should be safe here. It's unlikely that anyone is going to find you here."

Hale snorted. "Stephanie and I might not get shot, but I'm willing to bet we're going to pick up a couple of dozen diseases that haven't even been discovered yet."

The four of them got out of the car and entered the safe house.

"Wow," Stephanie said, when the lights were turned on and she was able to see the dismal interior of the house, "it's hard to believe the inside is even more pathetic than the outside."

Fasset chuckled. "It's not much, but we've got two officers stationed outside. If you'd rather we spent the money on a couple of throw rugs, I can send them home."

Hale grinned. "Point taken."

They went through the house quickly, and when they were done, Darley went and stood by the front door.

"We've got a couple of men stationed outside. I'm positive that no one knows that you're here, but we want to be on the safe side."

"We appreciate that," Hale said.

"We'll be going now. Get some rest and we'll stop by tomorrow to see if there's anything else we could be doing to get closer to the people behind everything that's going on."

***

Lying in bed, staring up at the ceiling, Hale desperately tried to get to sleep, but he couldn't shut his mind down.

There came a soft knock at his door.

"James?   Are you awake?" came Stephanie's voice.

Hale turned on the light and threw his pants on.   He put on his shirt and opened the bedroom door.

Stephanie stood there, and there was an expression on her face that made him nervous. "Can I come in?" she asked.

Hale moved to one side, and Stephanie went to sit down on the edge of the bed.

"What's going on?" he questioned.

She looked everywhere but at him. "James, I was thinking that...well, what I mean is that..." she started and then fell silent.

Hale frowned. "What am I missing here?   If you've got something to say, Stephanie, just come right out with it. After what the two of us have been through, the last thing in the world you need to do is be coy."

She met his gaze this time, and there was a look in her eyes that Hale recognized, and he slowly shook his head.

"We were nearly killed, James," she said, softly.

He nodded. "Yeah."

"There's a chance that we might not even come out of this alive, you know," she said, giving him a direct look.   "At times like this, a girl really appreciates everything that she has."

Hale found his heart racing. "Stephanie, when a person's been through a traumatic situation, they sometimes find themselves acting out on behavior that they wouldn't normally do.   It's a kind of stress-relieving mechanism the body produces."

"What do you think of me, James?"

"I think that you've a very attractive, very intelligent young woman," he said, wishing that she'd stop looking at him so intently.

She regarded him in silence for a long moment.

"What else do you think of me?" she asked.

"Um -- you're very polite," he said, wishing that this conversation weren't happening. "You also have extremely good posture."

She stood up and came over to stand directly in front of him. "Do you find me attractive, James?"

He wondered if she could hear the pounding of his heart. "Stephanie, right now, you're thinking that you're feeling something but it isn't real. It's a fantasy emotion that's being caused by the fact that we're in a very stressful situation. Your mind is trying to distract you from the situation by giving you another direction to go."

"You didn't answer my question," she pointed out.

Hale sighed.

"You're not listening to a word that I'm saying."

"Stephanie, right now, I'm not sure that this is the best time for you and I to be acting out on something that might turn out to be a very bad idea."

She raised one eyebrow. "So, you think that this is just because of what we've been through?" she asked.

He nodded. "Definitely."

"Ever since I've been old enough to understand what it is that I really want, I've wanted you. I've kept my feelings to myself because I didn't want there to be any weirdness between you and I. But, now that I see it's possible that I'm not going to survive, I wanted you to know how I felt about you."

Hale licked his lips.

He was having a hard time concentrating.

"If I ask you something," she said, softly, standing close to him, "will you answer me honestly?"

He sighed.

"Yes," he said, and it seemed as if his voice came from a total stranger.

"Are you attracted to me?" she asked.

He stared into her eyes.

"Yes," he finally said.

"Then, would you mind telling me why we're even having this conversation when there's a bed right over there that could be put to good use?"

"We're having this conversation because we're in the middle of finding out who killed your father -- and because until we're out of this mess, neither one of us is really capable of handling things rationally. If we just jumped into bed together, the only thing that would happen is someone -- probably both of us, in fact -- would get hurt."

She frowned. "What are you saying?"

"I'm saying that we need to see how things turn out here before we start working on whether or not we've got a future together."

Stephanie stared at him for a long moment, and she slowly nodded. "Fine. I should have known that's how you were going to react. And I'll tell you that I'm going to do exactly what you said. I'm going to play it the way that you want. And when this is over, I want you to know that I'm going to be coming back to you one night and I'm going to make the same offer to you, and if you turn me down then, you're going to be the stupidest man who ever lived."

CHAPTER TEN

The ringing of his cell phone brought Hale to wakefulness.

For a moment, he was completely disoriented. A few moments ago, he'd been caught in the middle of a strange dream -- a dream that involved him and Stephanie and a lack of clothing.

The phone continued to ring and he reached over for it. "Hello?"

"James?"

"Rouseeau! I've been trying to get in touch with you but I kept getting your voice mail. What the hell happened?"

There was a pause.

"Someone is trying to kill me," came the frightened voice.

"The same person who killed Claire?"

"Yes," Rouseeau whispered. "The same people killed Claire."

Hale tossed the covers to one side and started to get dressed. "What the hell is going on here?"

"It wasn't supposed to turn out this way, James. It really wasn't. I'm an archeologist, for Christ's sake! This isn't the way that my world is supposed to be."

"Why did Claire get killed?"

"For the same reason that they want me dead -- she knew the secret. It cost her her life."

"What secret? What the hell are you talking about?"

There was a pause.

"Not over the phone. I have to see you in person, James. I have to meet with you."

Hale sighed. "I wish I knew what to do, Rouseeau. On the one hand, I want to trust you, but right now, I'm not sure that I can trust anyone."

"James, you've known me for years. I might be an egotistical showboater when it comes to archeology. I won't deny that. I'm no killer, though -- and the people who are behind it want me dead because of what I've uncovered."

"Tell me who they are."

"I have to see you in person. If I tell you who's behind it, you'll have no incentive to help me out."

"It sounds like you're blackmailing me to get my help."

"I'm just playing the odds, James."

Hale sighed. "Tell me where you are."

"You're coming?"

"I'm coming."

"I need you to come alone, James. No police."

"If you're in trouble, let me -- "

"I think the police might be involved. No police."

Hale sighed.

"Fine. Tell me where you are -- and I'll come alone."

***

Ten minutes later, Hale found himself sneaking down the hallway of the safehouse.

Glancing into the dining room, he saw that both of Darley's watchmen were quietly sleeping, and he shook his head in wry amusement.

"I feel so much safer with these two on the job," he muttered, moving quickly to the front door.

Hale paused in the doorway and looked back, down the hallway from where he'd emerged. He debated whether or not to wake up Stephanie and tell her what was going on, and decided against it.

She'd want to come with him, and Hale couldn't risk having her walk into a trap.

He went outside.

Luckily, the driveway sloped upwards, so all he had to

do was get into his Renault and release the parking brake, coasting down to the road below.

Once he was on the road itself, he started the car and drove off to the destination that Rouseeau had given him.

On the one hand, Hale wanted to believe that the man he'd known for years was actually in trouble and that the two of them could join forces to get to the bottom of things. But, there was a part of him that wasn't so sure.

It's funny how a couple of days can change a man, he thought. *A week ago, I would have gone running to Rouseeau's aid without a second thought, and now I can't help but wonder if the man wants to kill me.*

Driving down the road, Hale tried to distract himself from his nervousness over walking into a trap with thoughts of Stephanie.

He couldn't deny that he had thought about the two of them in the past, and when she'd come to him and told him how she felt, it had almost been like a dream come true. But, Hale knew that she wasn't exactly the most worldly person out there and right now, she was very vulnerable.

He couldn't take advantage of her insecurities.

Of course, there was a chance that what she felt for him were the real emotions -- and if that was the case, he knew that he had to give the two of them a chance.

But, that was down the road.

Right now, he had to concentrate on getting to the bottom of the mess they were caught in. Until Aaron's killer or killers were brought to justice, they wouldn't be safe.

Hale saw the turnoff to the road that Rouseeau had given him, and he turned down it, desperately hoping that he wasn't walking into a trap.

***

Fifteen minutes later, Hale was ready to leave.

He was parked in front of an old farmhouse that looked as if it had been unoccupied for years. Rouseeau had told him that he would be there, but Hale was beginning to think that something had happened to Rouseeau, too.

He thought about everything that was going on, and he realized that coming to a meeting like this without having any kind of weapon had to be one of the most stupid things that a man could do.

Then again, Hale didn't like weapons very much. Years ago, his father had tried to teach him how to use a handgun, but the lessons hadn't gone well.

Hale hated guns.

Suddenly, a car approached, and Hale waited until it was parked across from him and a lone figure emerged.

He relaxed when he saw Rouseeau coming towards him.

Hale emerged from his car. "I was beginning to get worried about you," he said.

Rouseeau looked around, nervously "I've been watching you for a few minutes," he admitted. "I had to make sure that you were alone."

Hale frowned. "You think that I'd lie to you?"

"Of course not. But, there was a good chance that you might have been followed. The people that we are dealing with here are both dangerous and crafty. They didn't get to where they are by playing nice."

Hale shook his head. "I'm so sick of all this cloak-and-dagger nonsense. So, did I pass the test? Was I followed?"

Rouseeau chuckled."No, you weren't."

"So, does this mean that you'll tell me what the hell is going on?"

"It's about a denarius coin, James."

Hale stared at him. "You're telling me that all of the crap that I've been going through is over an ancient coin? You'll have to do better than that."

Rouseeau laughed softly. "Oh, I can do better than that. You see, the coin in question was held by one very special person."

Hale's eyes widened.

"Wait a minute -- you're not suggesting that you've managed to find Jesus' denarius."

"That's precisely what I'm telling you. This is the coin that Jesus held when the Pharisees and the Herodians tried to trick him. It's the coin that He held when He said, 'Give to Caesar what is Caesar's and give to God what is God's."

Hale's mind was reeling. This coin was the stuff of legend, and for many archeologists, it was considered more valuable than the Holy Grail.

"How do you know that it's the coin?"

Rouseeau brushed the question aside. "I'll get to that in a while. What do you think such a coin would be worth?"

"There's no telling," Hale said.

"It would be worth millions, wouldn't it?"

"Probably. Where is the coin now?"

"Gone -- taken by the person who killed Claire and who now wants me dead."

CHAPTER ELEVEN

Rouseeau and Claire sat at a small table, going through some documents that needed verification, when there came a knock at the door. Both looked up and saw Montague standing there, a broad smile on his face.

In his hand, he held a photocopy of the diary that Rouseeau had given him.

"Well?" Rousseau asked. "What do you think?"

Montague stared at him, shaking his head in amazement. "I think that this might well be the most important find of your lifetime."

Rouseeau nodded. "I think that you might be right. Are you upset that you didn't come along with us on this dig?"

"Believe me, if it had been remotely possible, I would have been there. Unfortunately, I had some more pressing business that I couldn't get out of."

"Your loss."

Montague went over to the two seated archeologists. "Where is the coin right now?" he asked.

Claire moved some papers, revealing an ancient coin protected by a thick plastic envelope.

Montague stared at it in amazement. "Are you telling me that you've got that coin out in plain sight? It should be locked away in a bank vault, at the very least."

Rouseeau chuckled. "I'm afraid that I'll never learn to be quite as paranoid as you, my friend. Besides, coins can be stolen out of bank vaults, too."

Montague shook his head. "If I live to be a thousand, I'll never understand someone like you. You're always out there, thinking the best of people -- even though the evidence of the world around you should prove otherwise."

"If you're talking about the way that the bad news seems to be the only thing out there, I'm not naive enough to believe that the world is a wonderful place to be in -- but I also know that it's not quite the house of horrors that others might think it is. The bad news gets more press because that's what makes people tune in. It's human nature."

"Be that as it may, who are you using to auction the coin? I'm thinking you could probably get the most out of Sotheby's."

"Yes, well, we're not looking at auctioning it, I'm afraid," Rouseeau said.

"You have a private buyer, then?"

Claire spoke up. "The coin and the diary will be given to the museum. This way, the customer traffic will go through the roof -- and we'll be able to pay for some much-needed renovations."

Montague stared at her. "You can't be serious!"

"Why not?"

"Are you kidding? You're standing there, on the brink of what is sure to be the most incredible archeological find of the century, and you want to just give it away to a museum. Tell you what -- you give me the word and I'll make one phone call that will get you ten million dollars."

Rouseeau laughed. "Montague, you'll never change! To you, archeology is all about finding something rare and making a lot of money off of it. To me, it's all about finding out about our pasts and sharing it with the rest of the world."

Montague opened his mouth, then closed it. "You are someone who will never understand what really matters in the world, I'm afraid."

***

Rouseeau finished with his story, and sighed.

"From what I've been able to gather, Montague must have come back that night for the coin. He was probably caught by Claire, and he killed her in cold blood. When I returned to the house, the police were already there and I was able to find out what had happened."

Hale frowned.

"Why haven't you gone to the police?"

Rouseeau shook his head. "I can't."

"Why not?"

"I can't tell you that. Not yet, at least. When the time is right, I'll tell you everything that's going on, but right now, the less that you know, the better."

Hale shook his head.

"This whole thing -- it's absolutely unbelievable. How the hell did you get mixed up in something like this, Lionel?"

Rouseeau sighed. "It's amazing how human greed can affect a person so deeply. I watched someone I trust kill a friend in cold blood -- all for the sake of money."

"Yeah, well, if we don't get to the bottom of this, there are probably going to be more deaths, Lionel."

***

The green SUV pulled up in front of the safe house and quickly cut the lights and shut down the engine.

After a moment, the doors opened, and two men emerged -- Brandon Stone and Lenny Carpenter. Each man held a silenced automatic, and the two of them approached the front door.

"I'll get it," Stone said, taking a picklock from his pocket and slipping it into the lock.

Moments later, the door was unlocked and the two men went inside.

Moving quickly, they went to the living room, where they quickly dispatched both police officers, who had just begun to awaken to the danger they were in.

The bullets tore into them with silent and deadly

accuracy.

"The bedrooms," Stone said.

They went down the hallway and kicked open the doors to the bedrooms, each of them taking a separate room.

Stone went into one room, Carpenter into the other.

A few moments later, both men came back into the hallway, and the look of disgust on both their faces spoke volumes.

"Gone," Stone said. "The window was open, but there was no sign of anyone."

Carpenter nodded.

"Same here."

"This isn't good."

"Yeah, well, we can kick ourselves later. Right now, we need to get the hell out of here before the cops call in to check on the two we wasted."

"No argument here," Stone said, and the two of them headed for the front door.

***

Stephanie, lying beneath the bed in one of the rooms, couldn't believe that the two killers hadn't heard the pounding of her heart.

This had to be some kind of nightmare. In her waking life, there weren't men out to capture her – or worse. It just didn't make sense, and if she had woken up in her bed, right then and there, she'd have been one of the happiest women in the world.

But, there was no waking up from this nightmare.

She lay there, long after she'd heard the car engine start up and fade away into the distance. The last thing in the world she wanted to go was stick her head out and discover that one of them had been left behind in order to trick her.

When she was satisfied that she was truly alone, she

crawled out from under the bed.

Moving as quietly as she could, she went to the bedroom door and looked out into the hallway. From where she stood, she could see the front door was still open, and her gaze turned towards the living room.

She slowly walked down the hallway.

There was a loose board about halfway down the hallway. When she reached the spot, she shifted off to the left, and continued moving forward.

There was a part of her mind that wanted her to turn around, wanted her to avoid going and looking into the living room, but she knew that was out of the question.

Maybe the intruders hadn't killed them. Maybe the cops had been asleep and they hadn't wanted to risk anyone waking up, so they just let them alone.

That was what she tried to tell herself, as she approached the room.

They were speaking in normal voices, she told herself. They weren't afraid of anyone waking up -- because they knew that no one was going to wake up.

Stephanie looked into the living room.

It only took her a second to know that both police officers were dead.

She rushed back into the bedroom, shaking violently. Her hands fumbled the cell phone out of her pocket, and after three tries, she was finally able to press in Detective Darley's phone number.

As she waited for him to answer, one question went through her mind -- where the hell was James?

CHAPTER TWELVE

Darley stood in the doorway of the living room, looking at the bodies of his two fallen men.

What he was seeing was inconceivable. The men that he'd left behind were trained professionals. How the hell had both of them managed to get themselves killed? They should have been able to spot any threat coming and deal with it – yet, obviously, they hadn't been able to do so.

When he turned to Stephanie, there was a deadly coldness in his eyes that made her take a step backwards. He closed his eyes for a moment, and took a deep breath.

"This is inexcusable," he said, his voice tight. "I don't know who is behind this, but I'm not going to rest until I see them either behind bars for the rest of their lives -- or dead."

Darley turned and went into the kitchen. Stephanie followed.

"What the hell is going on here?" he asked, softly. "It's like I'm trying to figure out how to put together a puzzle where none of the pieces fit."

"Welcome to my world," Stephanie muttered.

He gave her a long look. "Do you understand what this means?"

"I'm not sure."

"There's no way that anyone outside of the department should have known that you were here."

"Obviously, someone did."

Darley gave her a long look "There is another explanation," he said.

"What's that?"

"Professor Hale doesn't seem to be anywhere to be found. That leads me to believe that there might be a connection between the men who came here to kill you and Hale."

Stephanie snorted. "You obviously don't have a clue as to the kind of man that James Hale is. The thought that you could even imagine James being connected to this for one minute makes me wonder how it is that you could possibly be a police inspector."

"Miss Miller, I know that you're very close to Hale, but you'd be amazed at how often a person can think they know someone only to find out that they don't know them at all."

She shook her head. "Not James."

Darley decided to let it go, and went on with another area of questioning. "Mind telling me how you managed to stay alive when both of my men were killed?"

"I was heading into the kitchen when I heard a sound coming from down the hall. I didn't even turn to look to see what it was. I just rushed back into the bedroom, opened the window, and then hid under the bed. I saw it in a movie once."

Darley nodded, impressed. "Quick thinking on your part. It saved your life."

At that moment, his phone rang. He looked at the Caller ID.

"It's Hale," he told Stephanie, as he answered the call. "Where the hell are you?"

"And I'm delighted to hear your voice, too, Inspector."

"Hale, where are you?"

"Right now, I don't want to get into locations, if you don't mind. I've got some information for you, Inspector."

"And I have some information for you, too. Two of my officers are dead and your girlfriend could have joined them."

"What the hell are you talking about?" Hale shouted. "I was under the impression that we were in a safe house. The last I heard, that usually means the location is secure."

Darley sighed.

"It looks like we might have been compromised."

"Is Stephanie all right?"

"For the moment, she's fine. But, I've got some serious questions that I want answered -- starting with where the hell you are and why you snuck out of here."

"I received a call from Lionel Rouseeau. He had something important that he needed to tell me and I went to meet with him."

"I want the two of you to come in right now. This situation is rapidly spiraling out of control and if it's not stopped, there's no telling what's going to happen."

"Listen to me, Darley. You know that your department is compromised. Someone in it is dirty -- dirty enough to want to kill me and Stephanie. Right now, the best thing for you to do is put Stephanie under your personal protection. I'm staying out here with Rouseeau, until I'm sure that things are under control."

"Hale, you need to get back here and -- "

The line went dead.

Darley shook his head, and gave Stephanie a long look. "That might be the most frustrating man I've ever met."

She gave him a wan smile. "Welcome to my world, Inspector. Is James all right?"

"I think so. He got a phone call from Lionel Rouseeau and he went out to meet him."

"What are we going to do now?"

"We're going to get you to a much safer place -- and then I'm going to keep digging into this mess and try to keep Professor James Hale from becoming a file in the morgue."

***

Rouseeau and Hale sat in the small hotel room that Rouseeau had adopted at his temporary headquarters. Hale had gone over everything that had happened, and each man was lost in his own thoughts.

Finally, Rouseeau stood and began to pace. The room wasn't large enough to allow him much space, however.

"So, what do we know? There have been at least two murders -- Aaron Miller and Claire. There was a playing card left by each body," Rouseeau said. "So, Montague is playing games, but to what end? It doesn't make sense."

Hale shrugged. "Maybe he's trying to match wits with the cops?"

Rouseeau shook his head. "That's not his style. If anything, he likes to be behind the scenes -- not out in the spotlight. There's something else going on."

"Like what?"

Rouseeau sighed. "I wish I knew."

"There was also a poem at Aaron's murder scene."

"The playing card -- what was it?"

"The King of Spades."

"Historically, the King of Spades has been used to represent King David. And the King of Diamonds was left at Claire's scene -- which is usually indicative of Julius Caesar," Rouseeau said. "I think there's something here, but I can't quite put my finger on it."

Hale nodded.

"I know the feeling. It's as if I'm on the verge of understanding it, and then it slips away."

Just then, his cell phone rang. Glancing at the Caller ID, he saw that it was Stephanie, and he sighed.

"It's Stephanie -- Aaron's daughter. She's going to want to know what's going on."

"Do you trust her?" Rouseeau asked.

Hale nodded.

"With my life."

"Then perhaps we should bring her on board. The more people that we've got trying to unravel this, the more likely it is that we'll get to the bottom of it."
***

Stephanie went over to Darley's car and shook her head. "I wasn't able to reach him."

The police officer sighed. "He's not making things easy. There are some people out there who might think that he had something to do with what's going on -- just from the way that he's acting."

Stephanie shook her head. "No. Absolutely not."

Darley sighed. "If I don't get to the bottom of this mess quickly, there's going to be hell to pay. The only suspect I have is a man that I'm convinced is innocent."

"There is something that you need to do," she said.

"What's that?"

"You need to find out where the traitor in your department is."

Darley's features hardened. "If anyone had told me that I'd find myself in a position of having to investigate my own people, I would have thought they were crazy. I've always been able to trust the men under me."

She gave him a long look.

"There's a lot of money being tossed around in this," she said, "and money has a way of making people do stupid things."

Something in her tone caught Darley's attention.

"Does that have anything to do with Hale?" he asked.

"What are you talking about?"

"You said that money has a way of making people do stupid things," he said, "and from the expression on your face, it was more than just something to say."

She shook her head.

"It's nothing."

"Let me be the judge of that."

Stephanie shrugged. "It really isn't anything. There was a period of time when my father and James had a little bit of a falling out. James was going through a rough period, and he needed money. He was willing to do a couple of things that were borderline unethical, but when my father found out about it, he and James got into a real big fight. In the end, though, James came around and didn't go through with it."

Darley gave her a long look.

"You don't think something like that is important?" he asked.

Stephanie shook her head. "No. That was a different James."

"You'd be amazed at how people can fool you, Miss Miller. Keep that in mind."

Just then, Darley's cell phone rang, and he glanced over at Stephanie.

"I'd better take this," he said, heading towards the house.   "Darley here."

Stephanie watched as he went into the house, and then she began to walk quickly down the driveway.

CHAPTER THIRTEEN

Hale and Rouseeau sat at a table in a small, nondescript restaurant. Both men had glasses of wine in front of them.

Rouseeau looked around at the patrons, and sighed.

"Look at them, James -- enjoying themselves, living their lives the way that they want. Hard to believe that just a couple of days ago, I was one of those people."

Hale sipped his wine. "I'm right there with you, Lionel."

"There was a time when I thought that being an archeologist was one of the most boring professions around. Now, I'm seeing it in a whole new light."

At that moment, Hale caught sight of Stephanie entering the restaurant.

She looked around and spotted him.

The two men rose as she approached the table, and Hale gave her a quick embrace.

"How are you?" he asked.

She shook her head. "I've been better. After all, while you've been out here doing God knows what, I was back at the so-called 'safe house' being extremely unsafe."

Hale grimaced. "I'm sorry about that. If I had thought there was the slightest chance that you would have been in danger, I never would have left you by yourself."

Stephanie sighed. "Actually, you probably would have dragged me along with you."

Rouseeau cleared his throat and Hale nodded.

"Stephanie Miller, this is Lionel Rouseeau. Lionel, this is Stephanie -- Aaron's daughter."

Rouseeau gave her a sympathetic look.

"I'm sorry about your father."

"Thank you," she said.

Hale looked towards the door to the restaurant.

"You weren't followed, were you?'

She shook her head. "No. I got a lift from a couple of teenagers who were driving down the highway past the so-called 'safe house.'"

Hale grinned. "Darley's going to love that."

Stephanie nodded.

"Oh, he is. He's driving himself nuts with this case, and he's no closer to solving this than when he began."

Rouseeau made a disgusted face.

"In the past, I've learned that when you rely upon the authorities to do anything, you'd best brace yourself for a disappointment. I'm afraid that if we're going to get anywhere with this case, we're going to have to handle it on our own."

"What do you suggest?"

"I have a motel room not far from here. I didn't want to meet James there until I was sure that I would be safe."

Hale raised his eyebrows.

"Excuse me? Are you implying that you thought I might be the killer?"

Rouseeau gave him a steady look.

"You and I both know that we're dealing with some powerful forces right now, and the smart thing to do is play it safe. I just had to make sure that you weren't part of it."

"And what convinced you?"

Rouseeau nodded towards Stephanie.

"The girl. With her being involved, I knew it couldn't be you. No matter what else might change about you, James, you would never put a woman's life in danger."

***

Looking around the motel room where Rouseeau was staying, Hale slowly shook his head. "If anyone had ever told me that you'd be hanging out in a place like this, Lionel, I'd have thought they were out of their mind."

Rouseeau glanced around the disgusting surroundings -- at the stained bed, the cracked walls, the obscenities carved into the nightstand and sighed. "I decided that if I were going to be on the run, my safest bet would be to be in a place where I wouldn't normally be found."

Hale chuckled. "Well, congratulations on finding this place, because no one who knows you would think of looking for you here."

Stephanie gingerly sat on the edge of the one chair, as if afraid of contracting some kind of disease. "Instead of talking about how many stars this motel is going to get, can we start trying to figure out what the hell is happening here?"

Rouseeau nodded. "You're quite right, Stephanie. Let me fill you in on where we are."

Hale listened as Rouseeau explained everything that had been happening, and Stephanie listened carefully. When he was done, she said, "This coin that you're talking about."

"The denarius."

"Right -- how positive are you that it's the real deal?"

He nodded.

"Good question. The coin has an impeccable lineage -- more than anyone could possibly have hoped for. Apparently, it was obtained by a servant of a wealthy man. In all likelihood, this servant was an early follower of Jesus. He made sure that the coin was handed down through the generations with a parchment detailing how he had come to have it."

She nodded.

"James told you about the playing cards, then -- and the poem?"

Rouseeau turned to Hale, one eyebrow raised.

"Poem?"

Hale nodded.

"There was a poem left by Aaron's body. It read: 'Jesse / The roots / The Shepherd / Father of all greatness.'"

"And which card was left?"

"The King of Spades."

Rouseeau frowned.

"Interesting. The King of Spades would refer to King David.   Jesse was the father of David.   David was a shepherd."

"But when we put them all together, what the hell do we get?"

Rouseeau shook his head.

"I don't know, actually."

Hale sighed.

"I know that whatever it is that we're looking for is right under our noses. We're just overlooking it."

"Well, I hope we find out what it is before too much longer," Stephanie said, "since I've got a feeling that time is running out."

***

Inside the elegant home designed by renowned architect Francois Beauclaire, Pierre Merrill entered the drawing room.

A handsome man in his early fifties, Merrill was one of the wealthiest men in Europe, with holdings that ran the gamut from oil refineries to coal plants to nuclear generators.

His beautiful wife, Juliette Merrill, reclined gracefully on a couch, and gave him a warm smile.

"Who was on the phone, dear?"

Merrill turned to her.

"It was our friend."

"And -- ?"

Merrill went to a cabinet and placed his hand upon a recessed plate off to one side. There was a "snick" sound, and a hidden door slid open, revealing a chalice.

He stared at it with affection. "The Wishing Cup of Tutankhamen. It might well be the most expensive object in my collection -- and the one piece that I wouldn't ever part with. For thirty years, this cup has been mine -- through golden times and through the darkest of storms. I've seen it grant many a wish and I've felt the power that it contains."

"He wants the cup?" she asked, astonished.

Merrill nodded.

"Yes."

"Naturally, you told him that was out of the question," she stated.

Merrill chuckled.

"I'm afraid that I might have put it a bit stronger than that," he admitted. "Then again, our friend was being rather rude about the whole thing. When he realized that I wasn't going to sell it to him, he became abrasive. I have a feeling that our friendship is over."

Juliette made a worried face.

"I think that you might want to make sure that our security is tightened, then. He's the kind of man who might -- "

At that moment, Stone and Carpenter entered the room.

"He's the kind of man who might hire killers to handle his problems," Stone said.

Merrill and Juliette stared at the intruders. Without thinking, Merrill went over and stood in front of his wife, as if to protect her.

"What do you want?" Merrill asked, his voice shaking, his face pale.

Stone sighed. "I'm afraid that you probably already know the answer to that," he said, looking at the exposed Wishing Cup.

Merrill nodded. "Of course. You can have it. It's not

worth dying -- "

Stone fired two bullets into him, and he fell to the floor, dead.

Carpenter shot Juliette before she could scream.

Stone glanced at him and nodded.

"Nicely done. I'm sure she didn't even know it was coming."

"That was the plan." Stone looked around the drawing room. "You know, it's interesting that this man was blessed with so much money, and yet, when our employer wanted to buy something from him, he didn't want to sell it. What do you think that says about the man?"

Carpenter shook his head. "I don't know."

"It says that he was greedy. Greedy people never seem to profit, you know. They always wind up getting done in by their greed. It's inevitable."

Carpenter took a playing card from his pocket and gently laid it on Merrill's chest. "Just grab the cup and let's get out of here."

Stone shrugged. "It must be nice to live in that head of yours. Everything is all business, isn't it?"

"Just get the cup."

***

Darley was at his desk, going over some budget reports he'd been putting off while working on the Miller murder, when Fasset walked in.

"The way that you work around here," he said, "you might as well just start sleeping in the office. Maybe we can get you a little shower or something."

Darley snorted. "Don't say that too loud, if the Commissioner hears you, he'll take you seriously -- and I'll make sure that we get one set up for you, too."

Fasset chuckled. "I just got a report that there's been a

murder over in the St. Elysee area. I guess we'd better go and see what's going on."

Darley shook his head. "You can handle it. I'm up to my eyeballs in the Miller investigation."

"Husband and wife were shot -- and a playing card was left behind."

Darley looked disgusted. "Damn it!"

He grabbed his coat and flew out of the office, Fasset right behind him.

As they barreled down the hallway, Darley said, "This whole mess is getting out of control. So far, I've had the hotshots keeping their distance, but I'm pretty sure that I'm running out of time for that. They're going to be coming down on me, and they're going to want to have answers."

Fasset shook his head. "They can't expect miracles from you. Whoever is behind this is making sure that we're going off into a dozen different directions."

"Speaking of different directions," Darley said, when they reached the car, "any word from Hale?"

"Not that I know of."

"If we don't get to the bottom of this, the next murder that we investigate is going to be Hale's."

CHAPTER FOURTEEN

Darley and Fasset walked into Merrill's mansion, and both men were taken aback by the sheer opulence of the home.

Actually, calling it a "home" would have been an understatement. It was more like an exclusive hotel, and Darley found himself wondering why in the world anyone would want to live like that.

Fasset, as if reading his thoughts, looked around and shook his head. "Places like this give me the creeps," he said. "I can never imagine real people living like this. It just seems like something that you'd see staged in a movie or something."

"That's because rich people have too much time and money on their hands, and they spend a lot of both just wasting it."

The two men followed the sound of voices talking to what turned out to be the drawing room, where they found the crime scene team already hard at work.

Off to one side, a tall, slender man regarded the proceedings with a look of disapproval.

The detectives went over to him.

Darley flashed his badge, and said, "You're the one who called it in?"

The man nodded. "Yes, detective."

"And who are you?"

"I'm Farnsworth. I was Mr. Merrill's personal assistant."

"What happened?" Fasset asked.

"I came by to drop off some papers that I needed Mr. Merrill to sign. I knew something was wrong even before I went inside."

"Why's that?" Darley asked.

"The front door was ajar."

"Did you see anything out of the ordinary when you

went inside? Were there any suspicious cars or anything parked outside?"

Farnsworth shook his head. "Nothing."

"How long have you worked for Merrill?" Fasset asked.

"A little over five years."

"Any idea who might have wanted to kill him or his wife?"

"Mr. Merrill was a very powerful man. I'm sure there were people who wanted to see him get hurt. It's the way that most people are."

Darley looked around the room, and after a moment, he went over to the cabinet.

"What was in here?" he asked.

Farnsworth came over and stood next to him.

"That would have been the cornerstone of Mr. Merrill's collection -- the Wishing Cup."

"Never heard of it."

"Few people have. It was a goblet attributed to the Egyptian king, Tutankhamen. According to legend, whoever possesses the Wishing Cup would have all of their wishes granted."

"Yeah, well, looks like your boss didn't wish for a long life," Fasset said.

Darley turned to Farnsworth.

"Any idea where the cup went?"

"No, sir."

Darley turned to Fasset. "I think I've got to make a call."

Fasset rolled his eyes. "I still say that our boy Hale knows more than he's letting on."

***

Hale, sitting on the hotel bed, answered his cell phone,

after glancing at the Caller ID.

"What can I do for you, Inspector?"

Darley's voice came through, impatient and upset.

"Hale, where the hell are you?"

"I'd prefer to keep that information private for the moment."

"Is Stephanie Miller with you?"

Hale chuckled.

"Yes, she is. I imagine that you were a little upset when you realized that she'd decided to go off on her own."

There was a long pause.

"Hale, we've got a situation here and it would make it a lot easier on all of us if you'd just come on in and help us sort out this mess."

"I'd love to do that, but considering that the last time I put my faith in you, there were hired killers waiting to take me and Stephanie out, I think that I'll pass. On the other hand, though, if there's anything that I can for you over the phone, I'll be more than willing to help out."

"There's been another murder."

"Who was it?"

"Pierre and Juliette Merrill. Do you know them?"

Hale sighed. "I've heard of Pierre Merrill. He's a collector of sorts."

"From what we've been able to learn, it looks like Merrill and his wife were murdered and something called the Wishing Cup was stolen."

"Tut's Wishing Cup?" Hale said, surprised. "I'd heard that it was in the hands of a private collector, but I didn't realize that it was with Merrill. Come to think of it, though, that makes sense."

At that moment, the motel door opened and Rouseeau came in.

When he saw Hale on the telephone, he stiffened, but Hale held up a finger, and said,

"Inspector, let me get back to you. I want to check on something."

He hung up the phone.

Rouseeau glared at him. "Who were you talking to?"

"The police."

He frowned. "Why?"

"It was Darley. He called to tell me that Pierre Merrill and his wife were killed."

Rouseeau's eyes widened. "Dear God! When will this end?" he whispered. "Tell me something -- was there a playing card involved?"

Hale frowned. "I didn't even think to ask," he said, taking out the phone and dialing Darley's number.

It was answered on the third ring.

"Have you come to your senses, Hale?" Darley asked.

"Sorry to disappoint you, Inspector, but I'm not ready to throw in the towel just yet. I'd like to find out something, though."

"You want me to help you but you don't want to help me?" Darley said, skeptically.

"By helping me, Inspector, you'll be helping yourself -- and you know it."

There was a pause.

"What do you want?"

"Was there a playing card left at the scene?"

"It was the King of Clubs."

"The King of Clubs," Hale said, aloud.

Rouseeau raised his eyebrows.

"That would be Alexander the Great."

"Inspector, thanks for the help. I'll be in touch," he said, and quickly hung up before the police officer could get a word in.

Hale and Rouseeau exchanged confused looks.

"I'm lost here," Hale admitted. "On the one hand, we have what looks like a serial killing spree -- but there's definitely some other motive at stake. I just don't understand why we're dealing with such game playing."

Rouseeau nervously bit his lower lip, lost in thought. "If we have one card that symbolizes Julius Caesar and one card that represents King David and add to that a card that is supposed to symbolize Alexander the Great, it doesn't make sense."

"Unless we're trying to go into this too deeply," Hale said.

Rouseeau frowned. "What do you mean?"

"Let's say that the three cards just represent powerful influences from around the world," he said, thoughtfully. "Instead of them actually being clues, I think they're being used as calling cards -- sort of letting certain people know that there are some unstoppable forces at work here."

"But, the art objects that were stolen..."Rouseeau began.

Hale nodded. "Right. I think those were just taken out of greed. Then again, it could be much more than that. Think about it -- how hard would it be to sell those two objects?"

Rouseeau thought for a moment. "Personally, I would think they would be nearly impossible to sell. The minute they wound up being shopped around, you'd have the authorities coming down on you like an avalanche."

"Exactly," Hale said. "That means that it's possible this wasn't about greed. This was about possession. It was about having something that no one else did -- and thereby showing the extent of the power that the murderer has."

Rouseeau sighed. "If you're right -- and I suspect that

you might be -- there's nothing that we're going to be able to do. If Montague doesn't want to put those items on the market, there's no way that we're going to be able to nail him."

Stephanie spoke up, then. She'd been so quiet that both men had forgotten she was in the room with them. "We need to get to Montague before he gets to us. By the time he decides to take care of us, it's going to be too late."

Hale nodded. "You're right. As long as we remain in a reactive mode, we're going to be sitting ducks."

"What are you suggesting?" Rouseeau asked.

"We need to go pro-active."

"How?"

"We need to go to Montague and nail him."

Rouseeau shook his head.

"He's never going to walk into a trap, you know."

"He will if we can offer him something that he can't resist."

"Such as?" Rouseeau asked.

Hale grinned. "There's someone that I want you to meet."

***

Rouseeau glanced over at Hale, who was driving quickly through some congested traffic. After a particularly close call with a taxi, he said, "James, you might want to slow it down a bit."

Hale shook his head. "We've got to be on time. If there's one thing that Andre doesn't like, it's for people to be late."

"Exactly who is this guy that we're going to see?"

Hale chuckled. "Someone who might be able to get his hands on something that Montague will not be able to resist."

"Why don't you tell me what it is?"

"I'd rather you were surprised."

Rouseeau noticed that Hale had driven them into the part of town where most people didn't venture, and he suddenly understood why Hale had insisted that Stephanie remain behind.

"I guess this is why you wanted Stephanie back there," he said. "It looks like we're going into some rough territory."

Hale glanced over at Rouseeau, and there was a tight look to his face.

"Actually, I wanted Stephanie to stay behind so that someone would know where we were going -- just in case things went wrong."

Rouseeau frowned. "What kind of people are we dealing with here?"

"Let's put it this way -- Andre trusts me more than he probably trusts anyone on the face of this planet -- and he wouldn't hesitate to put a bullet in my brain if he thought that I was trying to put one over on him."

Rouseeau shook his head. "I'm beginning to wonder if it might not have been safer for me to just meet with Montague."

Hale chuckled. "Too late," he said, pulling up in front of a large warehouse. "We're here."

The two men emerged from the car, and went to a small door off to one side.

Three large men stood in front of the door, watching them carefully.

"I'm here to meet with Andre," Hale told the largest of the men. "I'm James Hale."

The men regarded him with cold eyes for a long moment, then stepped to the side, opening the door.

Hale and Rouseeau quickly went inside.

While the warehouse looked like an ordinary warehouse from the outside, on the inside, it looked like a state-of-the-art scientific laboratory. There were men in sterile white lab coats hunched over various machines or using different kinds of liquids on what looked to be stone artifacts.

A tall, gaunt man came over, then, and although he was smiling warmly, the smile never quite reached his cold, dark eyes.

He grabbed Hale's hand and pumped it furiously. "James, it has been too long!   How have you been?"

"Hello, Andre -- looks like business is booming here."

Andre nodded. "Times are good," he said, his eyes moving over to Rouseeau. "Lionel Rouseeau -- an honor."

He went over and the two men shook hands.

Rouseeau looked confused. "You know me?"

"Let us say that I know of you, rather -- and what I've heard impresses me. Your love of archeology is matched only by my love of wealth, and the two meet more often than you might think."

Hale nodded. "Speaking of which, did you get what I wanted?"

Andre turned to him. "I did, indeed," he said, and there was a strained tone in his voice. "You realize that if this were anyone else, James, I would never have agreed to this."

"Andre, I know that -- and I appreciate it. This means more to me than you know."

Andre went over to a small table, where an ornate wooden box rested. He opened it and removed a palm-sized object, which he took over to Hale, who held it reverentially in his hand.

Rouseeau frowned. "What's going on?" he asked.

"The Spear of Longinus," Hale said, softly. "This is the tip of the spear that pierced Christ's side as he hung on the cross."

***

After five minutes of driving in silence, Rouseeau finally spoke, staring down at the box in his lap.

"James," he finally said, in a strangled voice, "is this thing for real?"

Hale nodded, glancing over at him. "Definitely. It's been in Andre's possession since the beginning of 2000. I'm not sure where he managed to find it, and if there's one thing that I've learned about Andre, it's best not to ask any questions."

"But, the Spear of Longinus..." Rouseeau whispered, his voice quivering. "It seems beyond belief."

Hale chuckled. "I know. But the way that I see it, if I'm going to prove that Montague is the murderer, I'm going to need something that's going to pull him out of whatever hole he's hiding in. That means that I've got to offer him something that's irresistible."

"Why do you have the real Spear, though? Surely, you could just get by with a replica?"

Hale shook his head. "I can't risk it. I need for Montague to know that I've got the real Spear. The moment that we left, Andre went to work and made sure the word hit the streets as to what we've got in our possession."

"I can't believe that this friend of yours would just hand it over to you."

Hale chuckled. "It wasn't that he wanted to, that's for sure -- but at the same time, he owed it to me. I'm the one who originally found the Spear for him, after all."

Rouseeau stared at Hale. "You had the Spear in your possession originally?"

He nodded. "Yes."

"Why in the world wouldn't you turn it over to a museum, then? The historical value of this object alone is -- "

"The moment that it wound up in a museum, the

Vatican would have its agents coming down and confiscating it. Believe me, when it comes to religious artifacts, I know how efficient those people are. It would be locked away forever."

"Your friend Andre seems to have done well keeping it hidden, too," Rouseeau pointed out.

Hale nodded. "He did -- but he has his reasons, too. You know the legend behind it, though?"

"It was the Spear that cut open Christ when he was being crucified. It's said that his blood on it gave it incredible powers."

Hale nodded.

"I've got it on very good authority that those powers are real -- and they are not all bad. It's been used as a healing tool, as well -- and Andre, believe it or not, has been instrumental in that."

"You seem to have some very interesting friends, James."

"You don't know the half of it," Hale said, pulling into the motel parking lot. "And now, let's see if we can't get the magic of the Spear to help lead Montague to us."

The two men went to the room and froze.

The door was ajar.

Hale turned to Rouseeau. "You might want to wait in the car."

"I'd rather stick with you, if you don't mind," he said, and with that, the two men entered the room.

It was obvious that there had been a struggle, and it was obvious that Stephanie was nowhere to be found.

Hale went through the main room and the bathroom, and there was no sign of the girl anywhere.

A cold chill went through him.

Rouseeau shook his head.

"Before you start thinking the worst, it's possible that she went out for something. Maybe she -- "

Hale's cell phone rang.

"Hello?"

"Hello, James," came Montague's voice. "I stopped by your motel room a little while ago to pay you a visit, but it looks like I missed you. However, on a brighter note, I did bump into Aaron's daughter, and I have to admit that I'm impressed with the company that you've been keeping."

Hale's hand gripped his phone and he did his best to keep his voice under control. "Listen to me, Montague, and listen good -- if anything happens to Stephanie, I will find you and -- "

Montague cut him off, his voice cold. "Don't try to come across as the big, bad wolf, James -- it's not you. Unfortunately for you, however, it's a role that I'm very well familiar with, and one that I don't mind using to my advantage."

Hale took a deep breath. "What do you want?"

"Ah, that's more like it.   What do I want? That's a very good question. I want many things, James. On the other hand, I suspect there's really only one thing that you want."

"I want Stephanie returned -- unharmed."

Montague laughed. "Exactly what I expected you to say.   Now that we know what you want, we need to figure out what it is that I want."

"Just get to it, Montague."

"I heard the most interesting rumor a little while ago. Do you know what it was?"

"I can guess."

"You've got the Spear of Longinus, don't you?"

Hale sighed. "Yes."

There was a long pause.

"James, you never cease to amaze me. Not only have you known where the Spear was, all these years, but you actually managed to get your hands on it. That's astonishing."

"Save it, Montague. You know what I want."

"I'm assuming that you want to trade the girl for the Spear."

"Yes."

"I think that can be arranged."

Hale took a deep breath. "I want to talk to her."

There was a pause.

"I'm afraid that's not going to be possible. It was a little more difficult to get Miss Miller to come with us than I had hoped, and there was a slight amount of force used."

Hale's face turned red with rage. "If anything's happened to her, Montague, I'll – "

"You won't do anything, James, and we both know it. You're not the type. However, you can rest assured that she's fine. Oh, she might wake up with a slight headache, but that'll be the worst of it. Now, all you and I need to do is figure out where to meet."

"I'll pick the spot," Hale said.

"Afraid not. I have a feeling that if you choose the location, I'll find myself knee-deep in police officers, and that's something that I'd rather not deal with. Tell you what – I'll call you when I find the right location, and you can meet me there. That way, I can make sure that there are no tricks."

"But, that's – "

The line went dead.

Hale hung up his phone and turned to Rouseeau. "He's holding all the damned cards," he said, "and all we can do is wait for him to slip up – if he ever does."

***

Rouseeau watched as Hale paced back and forth yet

again, and he finally said, "James, you need to stop that. I'm getting a sore neck from watching you."

Hale forced himself to sit down on the edge of one of the beds, and sighed. "I can't believe that things have gotten this out of control. If I'd thought for one minute that Stephanie would have gotten into trouble, I never would have agreed to have her come with me."

"Stop beating yourself up, my friend. You couldn't have known things would come to this. Besides, unless I'm mistaken, she's the one who came to you to help her find out what happened to her father."

"The moment that he turned up dead, I should have walked away from this."

Rouseeau shook his head.

"That's not the kind of man that you are. Your friend was murdered, and I know you well enough to know that you're not going to rest until the people responsible are brought to justice."

"Sure -- unless Montague winds up killing Stephanie, too."

"I don't think that he'll do that. He's not a stupid man. He knows that she's his ticket to getting his hands on the Spear -- and to possibly get away with his crimes. If he were to kill her, that's one more charge they'll have against him."

Hale took out his phone and punched in a number.

"Who are you calling?"

"Darley and Fasset. If Montague calls me, I'm going to want them there for backup."

Rouseeau frowned. "Do you trust them?"

He sighed. "Right now, I don't think that I have much choice in the matter. I'm going to have to trust someone to be there if Montague decides that he's going to clear up all the loose ends at once."

After a few moments, he sighed and closed the phone.

"He's not picking up."

Hale's phone rang.

He picked it up, thinking that it was Darley, but instead, he heard Montague say, "I have a location, James."

CHAPTER FIFTEEN

Thirty minutes later, Hale pulled off one of the main roads, moving along what appeared to be more of a path than an actual road.

He hated having a meeting in a place like this, but there was no choice in the matter. Montague was calling the shots, and that meant that Hale was going to have to jump through whatever hoops the man was going to put in front of him.

The car jounced around wildly, and Rouseeau shook his head.

"I think he's trying to kill us with concussions here."

Hale sighed. "He's probably watching us from a distance and making sure that we don't have anyone with us."

A few moments later, Hale came to a spot that had a large boulder off to the right side. He turned to Rouseeau and nodded. "This must be it."

He stopped the car, and remained behind the wheel.

Rouseeau gave him a curious look. "What are we waiting for?"

"I'm not too thrilled with being led out here in the middle of nowhere. I'm staying here until Montague gets in touch with us -- because I don't want to find myself getting shot."

At that moment, the cell phone rang, and Hale answered it. "Montague?"

There was a cold chuckle. "James, why on earth are you just sitting in the car? I would have thought that you'd want to get this over with so that you could be reunited with that lovely young girl of yours."

Hale found himself tightly gripping the steering wheel. "Where are you?"

"Right here," Montague said, and emerged from around the side of the boulder.

Hale opened the door and stepped out, box held tightly in his hand.

"Where's Stephanie?" he demanded.

Montague shook his head. "I'm afraid that I didn't want to bring her with me, James. You see, just on the off-chance that you were planning on doing something foolish, I thought that it would be best if I had something to use as leverage -- specifically, the girl. So, the way that this is going to work is you're going to hand the Spear over to me, and in turn, I'll call you in a few minutes and tell you where you can find your little friend."

Hale frowned. "And why should I trust you?"

"You shouldn't -- but you also have no choice. Right now, I'm the only game in town."

Shaking with barely contained rage, Hale tossed the box to Montague, who easily caught it.

"You've made a very wise decision, James."

"If this turns out that you're pulling something here, Montague, I'll -- "

Before Hale could finish, however, there was the sound of sirens and within moments, a police car came screaming up to the site, and Darley was out of the car before it was entirely stopped.

He had his gun drawn, and he had it aimed to Montague.

"Police!"

Montague turned to Hale, and his features were twisted in rage.

"You've made a serious mistake, James."

Hale shook his head.

"I didn't call them," he said, and gave Darley a confused look. "How the hell did you know where to find us?"

Darley nodded at Fasset.

"Fasset received an anonymous tip," he said.

Hale frowned, confused.

"I don't understand how that could be. The only person who knew about the meeting was Montague, and there would be no reason for him to -- " he began, and then his eyes widened as he looked over at Fasset.

The man stood next to Montague, and he had his weapon trained on Darley.

Before Hale could shout a warning, there were two quick shots and Darley fell to the ground.

Hale stared at Montague. "He's in on it," he said, stunned.

"Of course. Apparently, the salary of a police officer isn't enough to keep everyone on the straight and narrow," he said, and turned his attention to Hale's car. "You might want to come out and join the party, Lionel."

Rouseeau emerged from the car, and stood next to Hale. "By any chance, do you have a way out of this particular situation?"

Hale sighed. "Not at the moment."

Montague turned to Fasset. "I guess the smart thing to do here is to go ahead and kill these two, and then we'll come up with a scenario."

Fasset sighed. "I hate having to do this," he said, and turned his gun towards Hale.

A shot rang out.

Fasset's eyes widened in stunned amazement. He slowly dropped to his knees, and turned to where Darley stood, gun in hand.

Hale stared at the police inspector.

"What the -- ?" he started, and from the corner of his eye, he saw Montague grab Fasset's gun from the fallen police officer's hand.

Everything seemed to slow down. He saw Montague swing the gun around, saw the barrel come towards him, and there was a muzzle flash.

Rouseeau fell to the ground, crying out in pain.

Darley turned to Montague. "No!" Hale said. "Don't shoot -- !"

Too late.

Darley fired three rounds into Montague, and by the time he hit the ground, he was dead.

***

Hale paced the hallway in the hospital, and Darley watched him carefully. After a moment, Hale turned to him, and said, "You've been watching me like a hawk for the past ten minutes, Darley. What's going on?"

The detective sighed.

"I've been hoping to see something that might make me think that you're the person behind this nightmare, but it's obvious that you're not. The problem is, I don't know where the hell to start looking now. If anyone had told me that my own partner would betray me, I'd have said they were out of their mind."

Hale sat on the bench, and nodded. "I know how you feel. Everything about this case makes me think that I'm Alice and everything else is the Looking Glass. None of it makes sense. I mean, for Christ's sake, look at what your partner did to you. Why the hell would he do that?"

Darley shook his head.

"I don't know. At first, I was going to put it down to a question of money, but the more that I think about it, the more convinced I am that it goes deeper than that."

Hale gave him an intent look. "What do you mean?"

"Fasset may have had his faults, but he was a good cop. I'm sure of that. If he turned dirty, it wasn't for money."

"What would it have been for, then?"

Darley shrugged. "It could have been anything, I think. Montague took your girlfriend for leverage. Perhaps the same thing happened with Fasset."

Hale pondered that for a few moments.

"It's possible," he finally said. "If you really want to put pressure on someone, money isn't the way to go about it. But, if you've got leverage in a different area, that changes everything."

"That's the direction I'm going."

"Of course, you don't have any proof."

Darley gave Hale an intent look. "Fasset watched me put on the bulletproof vest that saved my life before we left. He knew that his shots weren't going to kill me. He also knew that I was going to kill him the moment that he turned his weapon on you."

Hale stared at Darley. "What the hell kind of people are we dealing with here who have that much power -- power enough to have a police detective sacrifice his life?"

"I don't know. Hopefully, we'll get some answers shortly," Darley said, watching as a white-coated physician came walking towards them.

When he was standing in front of them, the look on his face told them everything they needed to know.

"I'm sorry," he said, "but it doesn't look good. The patient named Rouseeau suffered a tremendous blood loss and he's not going to make it. The other man -- Montague -- is unconscious and there's been severe internal hemorrhaging. In all likelihood, he's not going to pull through."

Darley stood. "Doctor, we appreciate everything that you're doing, but it's vital that we get information from Montague. There's a woman's life at stake. We need to know what it is that he knows."

"I understand the gravity of the situation, but there really isn't anything that we can do. He's unconscious, and there isn't any way that we can bring him out of it."

Hale resisted the urge to scream in frustration.

"Thank you for everything, doctor," Darley said.

When the physician left, Hale turned to the detective and asked, "What now?"

"I think we should go to Montague's apartment and see if we can't get lucky and find something that might be useful."

Hale sighed, knowing they were going on yet another wild goose chase.

***

Half an hour later, Hale and Darley stood in the middle of the mess that had been Montague's apartment.

When they'd arrived, the front door had been smashed open.

Darley, gun drawn, went in ahead of Hale, warning the professor to "stay put until I give you the go-ahead."

He entered the apartment.

Five seconds later, Hale was right behind him.

Darley turned around and gave him an angry look.

"You don't believe in following orders very well, do you?"

Hale shrugged.

"I thought that I'd rather be around the man with the gun, rather than standing out in the open, where I might as well have a bull's-eye painted on me."

Darley sighed, putting the gun away. "It doesn't matter. Whoever was here is gone."

Hale looked around the apartment.

It had been completely trashed.

Cushions had been cut open, their stuffing spread all over the floor.   Books were thrown around, pages ripped out.

Anything that was breakable had been shattered.

Darley shook his head.

"Obviously, Montague had something that someone else wants. I wonder what the hell it was -- and I wonder if they got it."

Hale headed out of the living room area, and Darley followed him. "Where are you going?"

"The kitchen," Hale said. "I saw a show on one of the television channels about the best place to hide something from prying eyes is actually in the kitchen. Most people hide things in either the study or the bedroom, but that's where everyone always looks. The trick is to find a place that most people aren't going to think about."

The two men entered the kitchen.

It, too, had been trashed.

"I guess our visitors saw the same program," Darley commented.

Hale sighed. "It was worth a try."

There were pieces of mail scattered all over the place, most of which seemed to be bills. Hale knelt down and started going through them. Darley, meanwhile, opened cabinets and drawers.

"Do we have any idea what we're looking for?" Hale asked.

"Anything that might remotely provide us with some kind of direction to take, I guess."

Hale headed into the bedroom, while Darley opened the refrigerator, peering at the contents. He checked every jar and bottle, just in case something was hidden inside, but wound up drawing a complete blank.

Darley went into the bedroom, and surveyed the damage. Like everything else in the apartment, it had been totally trashed.

Hale shook his head. "Nothing."

Darley picked up a paperback copy of THE DA VINCI CODE from the floor, and chuckled. "It's nice to know that even sociopathic killers don't mind reading trash now and then."

Hale laughed. "I'm sure that Dan Brown would be thrilled to know that he's a hit among twisted serial killers."

Darley tossed the book down on the floor, and a piece of paper slid out from the pages where it had been resting.

The two men looked at each other and both reached for it at the same time.

Darley got to it first. He examined it and there was an excited look in his eyes as he told Hale, "It looks like it's a receipt for a warehouse rental.   It was dated two days ago."

Hale raised his eyebrows. "So, a couple of days ago, Montague decides to rent a warehouse. That would be right around the time that he would have seen that we were getting close to him, so this location might have something to do with everything that's going down."

Darley gave him a long look. "It   might   be   nothing, Hale."

"I know -- but right now, it's the only game in town, inspector."

"Let's go and see if we can't turn up something, then."
***

Forty-five minutes later, Hale and Darley found themselves outside what looked like an abandoned warehouse.

It was located in an industrial section of town that had seen much better days. The windows were boarded up, and there were several rusted out iron drums scattered around. There didn't seem to be any sign of life around the place.

Darley glanced down at the ground, and knelt beside a dark puddle. Putting his finger in it, he lifted it for Hale's examination.

"What is it?" Hale asked.

"It looks like it's motor oil -- and fresh."

"So, someone's been here recently," Hale said, looking around. There didn't appear to be any signs of life, with the exception of an old homeless man parked across the street. The filthy old beggar watched them for a few moments, then lifted a brown paper bag and took a long drink from it.

Darley took out his gun and went to the warehouse entrance. Hale was right behind him.

Going to the door, Darley cautiously pushed it open, then quickly ducked back. When it was obvious that no one was about to take any potshots at them, he went inside.

The inside corroborated what the outside had said -- it was deserted.

Darley went around carefully, looking for anything that might be a potential clue, but the place provided nothing. There was nothing on the floor but dirt, although there were several areas where the dirt had been disturbed.

Hale sighed. "It's obvious that someone's been here recently, but we have no idea who it might have been."

At that moment, there was a shadow in the doorway, and Darley swung around, gun in hand.

Both men relaxed when they saw it was only the old man from across the street.

Hale went over to him. "Do you know where the people who were in here went?"

The old man regarded him in silence for a few moments. Then, he said, "I might."

Hale's heart pounded. "Where?"

The old man's gray eyes regarded him carefully, and he leaned in close. Hale got a good whiff of the man, and he did his best to keep his distaste from showing on his face.

"It'll cost you a little bit," he said.

Darley came over, badge in hand. "You might want to rethink the shakedown, my friend. I'm sure you'd love to be a good citizen and help out the authorities."

The homeless man regarded Darley with resentment, and sighed. "There were three men -- big men. They've been here for a couple of days. There was a girl with them this morning, too."

Hale and Darley exchanged looks.

"Where did they go?" Hale asked.

"West. They had a van. They had the girl with them and I could tell that she didn't want to be there. One of them looked at me when they drove past, and I didn't like his eyes. They were mean eyes. I didn't like his eyes at all."

Darley noticed the look in Hale's eyes and went over to him. He rested a hand on the professor's shoulder. "I know what you're thinking, Hale. Don't do this to yourself."

Hale shook his head."This is my fault. What the hell was I thinking? I never should have let Stephanie get involved with this."

"We'll get her back," Darley said.

Hale turned to him with a haunted look in his eyes.

"The question is -- will there be a playing card next to her body?"

CHAPTER SIXTEEN

When it became obvious there were no answers to be found in the warehouse, Darley and Hale stopped in at a bar to have a couple of drinks. It had been Darley's idea, knowing that Hale was tearing himself up over what was happening with the case.

The two men were in a corner booth, a bottle of whiskey between them.

Off to one side, there was a young couple arguing in loud voices over whether or not the young man had been looking at some girl named Mandy, and across the bar, a group of men were loudly singing an off-key version of "Oops! I Did It Again."

Hale shook his head.

Darley poured whiskey into a glass and slid it over to Hale.

Hale downed it, wincing as it seared his throat. "What the hell am I doing here, Darley? I'm a damned history professor. I've got no business being mixed up in something like this."

"You're trying to avenge your friend's death."

"Sure, and look where I am -- I'll probably have gotten his daughter killed," Hale said, anguish in his voice. "If anything happens to her, I don't know what I'll do."

Darley sipped his whiskey. "Nothing will happen to her."

"You don't know that."

"I know that if whoever has her wanted her dead, she'd be dead already. Obviously, they're keeping her alive for a reason."

"They haven't contacted us since Montague. Maybe they've decided they don't need her any longer."

The police inspector shook his head. "More   likely,

Montague's situation has caused theirs to change. They're probably trying to decide how to proceed from here."

"I just don't understand how this could have happened. What the hell is going on?"

Darley sighed. "Welcome to my world, Hale. It's not a pretty one, is it? There are powerful people involved in this and when powerful people show up in a case, it always gets messy."

"How do you do it?"

"I just put my head down and bulldoze my way through the mess."

"Having been on the receiving end of your bulldozing head, Darley, I'll bet that you've taken a lot of blows to that thick skull of yours."

Darley grinned. "More than you know, Hale. For a college professor, you seem to be pretty damned stubborn, too."

"I come from a long line of hard-headed sonsabitches who don't give up."

Darley raised his glass. "Here's to the hard-headed ones."

They touched glasses.

"To the hard-headed ones," Hale said.

They downed their drinks, just as Darley's phone rang.

"Hello? This is he...when?...we'll be right there," he said, hanging up.

He turned to Hale, excited.

"That was the hospital. Montague's regained consciousness."

***

By the time that Hale and Darley arrived at the hospital, the sun was just setting.

They had to get permission from the attending

physician before they were allowed to move further, and it seemed as if the man was having a hard time being located. Hale and Darley quickly found themselves losing patience, and Darley was about to force the issue when a young physician approached them.

"I'm Doctor Bradley," he said. "I understand that you want to speak with my patient."

Darley spoke. "Yes, we do."

"I'm afraid that I really can't allow that. He's in a very fragile state right now, and he needs rest. I think that exciting him might – "

Darley held up a hand. "Look, doc, I understand where you're coming from, and I wish that I could go along with what you want us to do. But, there are lives at stake here and I don't have time to play games."

The doctor stared at him. "I'll give you five minutes."

"Thanks."

Entering Montague's room, they found the man looking pale and drawn. Hale thought that he looked like a man who wasn't going to survive.

Hale rushed over to him. "Where's Stephanie?"

Montague let out a weak chuckle. "For an archeologist, James, you're remarkably impatient."

"This isn't the time for games. Where is she?"

Montague was seized with a choking spell. It overtook his entire body, lasting for nearly a minute, and when it passed, he didn't seem to know that Hale and Darley were in the room. "It wasn't supposed to be like this..."he whispered. "Everything had been planned out...they always plan these things out..."

Darley went over, kneeling beside the bed. "Who always plans these things out?"

Montague blinked, surprised to find the police

inspector there. "You're not going to trick me that easily," he said. "I know what you're doing."

"What am I doing?"

"You could be one of their men. You're testing me."

"Listen to me," Darley said, softly. "There's been a change of plans. They want us to get the girl."

Montague turned to Hale. "They know about the Spear, James. They're going to want it now."

"I'll give them the Spear," Hale said. "I just want to know where Stephanie is."

"I thought I was smarter than them, James," he said, softly. "I was wrong."

Once again, he was seized with a coughing attack.

Hale went over, leaning over Montague's bed.

"Who is behind this whole stinking mess?"

Montague looked up at him and for a moment, a look of defiance appeared in his eyes.

"They're the men who lurk in shadows, James. They are the Illuminati, and they're going to kill you and the girl."

Hale grabbed him and Montague started coughing. Unlike the earlier spells, this one didn't seem to want to pass, and the door opened, with a large, stern-looking nurse appearing in the doorway.

She looked at Hale and Darley with disapproval. "You'll have to leave."

Hale shook his head. "I need more information. I'll just -- "

The nurse took him by the arm, firmly escorting him to the door. "Come back later. The patient needs rest."

***

Hale lay in bed in his hotel room, staring up at the ceiling.

He couldn't get any sleep. The moment he closed his

eyes, he saw Stephanie there, frightened and alone. She kept looking at him with reproach, and even though he hadn't done anything wrong, Hale couldn't escape this overwhelming sensation of guilt passing through him.

How the hell did this happen? How had things gone so incredibly wrong? He'd wanted to get to the bottom of Aaron's death, and now it looked as if he might have gotten Stephanie killed.

Hale pushed those thoughts out of his mind. Right now, he couldn't even begin to consider that.

Hale threw the covers to one side, just as his telephone rang.

"Hello?" he asked, sitting up, heart pounding.

"It's Darley," came the response, "and I need for you to come down to the station. There's someone here you need to talk to."

Hale's heart pounded. "What is it?"

"Just get on down here, Hale," Darley said, hanging up the phone.

Hale got dressed.

***

When Hale reached the police station, he was escorted to one of the interrogation rooms, where he found Darley waiting for him.

There was a man sitting there – short, squat, with a milky eye that seemed to move about on its own.

Hale frowned as Darley approached him.

"This is Lankers," Darley said, nodding at the man. "Lankers is someone who helps the police now and then."

Lankers nodded.

"You might say that we have an arrangement."

Hale stared at the man. "An informant?"

Lankers shook his head.

"Informants are narcs. I just get information sometimes and pass it along."

"Lankers can tell us where Detective Fasset spent a lot of his off-duty time."

Hale raised his eyebrows. "Can he?"

"Oh, yeah – I can tell you about Fasset the Asshole."

"Lankers and Fasset didn't always get along," Darley explained.

"I hate dirty cops – especially the ones that try to come across like they're better than me."

"You've known that he was dirty?" Hale asked.

"Yeah."

"But, you didn't tell Darley?"

Lankers stared at him as if he were an idiot.

"Didn't I just get through with telling you that I'm not a narc?"

"But – "

"Now that Fasset is dead," Darley explained, "Lankers decided that it might be a good time to come forward and tell us what he knows."

"I see."

"You want to know where Fasset hung out, right? It's a place called 'The Eye.'"

"A club?" Hale asked.

"It's a club – and it's more than that. It's got a whole lot of business in the back rooms taking place all the time."

"What kind of business?"

"The kind of business that most people don't want to talk about."

Hale looked over at Darley, who nodded slightly.

"Lankers always gives us good info."

Hale stood. "I think that we need to take a look at this club, then."

Lankers gave him a long look. "The people Fasset hung with – they're not the kind of people you want to piss off."

"I've got a feeling it's a little late for that," Hale said.

***

Montague opened his eyes as the door to his room opened.

It was dark outside, and the lights in his room were set to the lowest level.   For a moment, he couldn't make out any details of the man entering his room, other than the fact that he wore a white doctor's coat.

"More tests?" Montague asked, weakly.

The visitor didn't reply, but dipped his hand into his pocket.

When it emerged, there was a syringe in it.

Montague immediately reached for the nurse call button beside his bed, but before he could press it, a hand came down, jamming the needle into the side of his neck.

Darkness washed over him within moments.

***

Darley and Hale sat in the parked car across the street from The Eye, watching as a large bouncer guarding the front door decided who could enter and who couldn't.

As several young people went inside, Darley said, "I envy those kids, Hale. They have their whole lives ahead of them."

Hale snorted. "Sure – and they don't realize that the world they're growing up in is turning colder and darker by the minute. Human decency is a thing of the past and the wicked and corrupt are out there, calling all the shots. Meanwhile, these kids go around with their heads in the sand, just wanting to go out and have a good time."

Darley gave him a long look. "You've got to be the most depressing stakeout partner I've ever had."

"I don't understand why we don't just go in there right now."

Darley sighed.

"That's not how it's done, Hale. First, we spend a little time checking things out, getting a feel for the place."

"So far, the only thing I'm getting a feel for is what it's like to have a case of floating bladder syndrome."

"I warned you about drinking too much coffee."

"Yeah, I know – but I need to stay awake, and sitting here in the car, twiddling my thumbs isn't cutting it for me."

At that moment, headlights washed across their car, and they watched as a limo pulled up in front of the club.

"I wonder which airheaded celebrity is going to show up now," Darley muttered.

The driver got out and opened the back door.

Cheever emerged from the limo, and Darley and Hale exchanged looks.

"Things have just gotten interesting," Darley muttered.

Hale raised his eyebrows.

"Somehow, this doesn't look like the kind of place where you'd find Cheever."

"Lankers told us there was a lot of business that went on in the back rooms here."

"I don't think it's a coincidence that the club where Fasset spent a lot of his off-duty time just had Cheever drop in for a visit."

Darley nodded. "We're onto something here."

"What's our next move?"

"I think that we should – "

Darley's phone rang and he answered it. "Hello?...When?...I'll be right there...Do that for me, would you?...Yes..."

He hung up the phone and looked at Hale. "That was

the hospital."

"What is it?"

"Montague's dead. I'm going to head over and find out what went down."

Hale glanced at the club across the street. "I'm staying."

"I don't think that's a good idea. You should come with me and then we can – "

"Cheever's in there. I want to see who he's meeting with."

Darley glanced at the bouncer across the street and said, "You might not be able to get past him."

Hale opened his door. "Nothing ventured, nothing gained. Besides, I've talked my way into some of the most highly protected archeological digs in the world. I'm pretty sure I can get past that one man."

Darley looked dubious. "Maybe I should stay."

"Go to the hospital. Find out what's going on there. Find out if Montague said anything before he died. I'll see if I can't get something on Cheever."

Darley gave him a worried look. "Be careful in there."

"Why, inspector, if I didn't know better, I'd say that you were worried about me."

Darley makes a face. "I just don't want to have to fill out a mountain of paperwork, explaining how an American archeology professor managed to get himself killed in France."

Hale got out of the car, and stuck his head into the open window. "If I'm not here when you get back, send in the cavalry."

Hale went to the front of the club and watched as the bouncer gave him a cold look. He went to move past him, but a massive arm pressed across his chest kept him from going any further.

Hale's heart pounded.

"Sorry. This is a private club," the bouncer said, his voice surprisingly soft for someone so intimidating.

Hale stared at him.

The bouncer regarded him with cold, pale eyes.

Even though every part of him wanted to turn around and walk away, Hale knew precisely how to deal with the situation. He'd been in the same position before, usually when doing a dig on a government controlled site.

Hale nodded. "Tell you what -- tell Cheever that I came to meet him, as per his request, but I couldn't get in," he said, and turned around, walking away.

The hard part was in continuing to walk away without turning around.

"Hey!"

Hale turned and looked at the bouncer. "What can I do for you?"

"Mr. Cheever knows that you're coming?"

"Yeah."

"I'm not supposed to let anyone in that I don't know and Mr. Cheever always tells me when he's meeting with someone."

Hale shrugged. "Like I said, just tell Cheever I was here. He knows how to get in touch with me."

The bouncer stared at him for another moment, and then stepped aside, opening the door.

Hale stood there for a few seconds, then nodded at the bouncer and went inside, heart pounding so hard that he wanted to throw up.

Once inside, the loud music assaulted him, and he moved through the maze of bodies dancing and slamming into each other.

The lights were flashing strobe-fashion, and Hale found

a spot off to one side, where he could observe the crowd. He wondered how he was going to find Cheever in this place. There had to be a couple of hundred people around him.

A drunk slammed into him, then turned to glare at Hale. "Why don't you watch where you're going?" the man demanded.

Hale didn't want to make a scene, and he said, "Sorry."

The drunk continued to look at him and there was a dark fire in the man's eyes -- he wanted to fight.

Hale started to back away.

"That's all you got to say to me?"

"Look, I don't want any trouble," Hale said. "I'm sorry that I didn't see you and -- "

At that moment, Hale saw Cheever emerging from a door off to one side. As if sensing his gaze, Cheever turned to look directly at him. He started to head quickly towards the door.

Hale went to intercept him, but was intercepted himself when the drunk grabbed him. "Where the hell do you think you're going?"

"I need to see someone," Hale said, jerking himself free.

"The only thing you're going to see, asshole, is my fist coming at your face."

Hale pushed the man to one side, sending him into a crowded table. He moved quickly past the scene, but before he could get much further, he found a hand on his shoulder, jerking him around.

The bouncer stood there, and his fist was the last thing that he saw before darkness washed over him.

***

Looking down at Montague's body, Darley felt like putting his fist through the wall. He needed the man alive to tell him who was behind the mess that Hale was caught up in, and now that he was gone, the inspector didn't hold out much hope for getting to the truth.

"What happened?" Darley asked the heavy-set nurse who was wrapping the electric cord of one of the monitors around the base of the unit.

She shrugged. "He passed away during the night. That's how it happens. When the nurse's aide came in to give him his medication, she found he was already gone."

Darley frowned. "That's when you found out he was dead?" he asked.

She nodded. "Yes."

Darley went over to the monitor and nodded towards the body. "He was hooked up to this machine?"

"Yes."

"And when he died, wasn't an alarm supposed to go off?"

The nurse thought for a moment. "As a matter of fact, it is."

Darley turned the monitor around and examined the back. There were two wires that looked as if they'd been cut, and he slowly shook his head.

At that moment, the hospital room door opened and a uniformed officer came in. He was a young guy, looking as if he'd just graduated from the academy.

He held a police officer's uniform and a white lab coat.

"We found these in the janitor's cleaning cart," he said.

Darley sighed.

Taking out his phone, he made a call to the station to find out who had been assigned guard duty on Montague. He was patched through to Francois Collins, a new recruit who had been on duty.

"This is Francois," came a youthful voice.

"Inspector Darley speaking. You were on duty last night at the hospital, watching Montague, weren't you?"

"No, sir."

Darley frowned. "No?"

"No, sir.   I was relieved by another officer."

"Who was he?"

There was a pause.

"I don't remember his name," came the reply. "As a matter of fact, I'm not sure if he even gave it to me. He was tall, though, and looked like he was in good shape. Is something wrong?"

Darley shook his head.

"Incredible. Didn't they teach you anything in the academy? You don't just walk away from a post without authorization. That's the first thing they should have taught you."

There was another pause.

"With all due respect, Inspector Darley, he had authorization."

"Who signed it?"

"The Chief Superintendent."

A cold chill went down Darley's spine. From where he was standing, it looked like whoever the assassin had been, he had either used a forged authorization document -- or else, he had actually been provided with genuine authorization, and if that was the case, the implications were staggering.

***

When Hale opened his eyes, he found himself in a barren room, dimly lit from a single light bulb high overhead. There was a single door to one side, and the floor was concrete.

He groaned and slowly rose to his feet.

Things were a little hazy, but he managed to remain

standing. When he touched his nose, he winced at the pain that shot through him, and he slowly shook his head.

"It always looks so easy in the movies," he muttered.

Hale went over to the door and tried to open it. He wasn't surprised when he discovered that it was locked.

"Ah, Professor Hale," came a voice from a small intercom that he hadn't noticed upon first regaining consciousness. "I'm glad to see that you're up and about."

The voice was cool and cultured, with the faintest trace of what might have been a British accent.

"Where am I?" Hale demanded. "Who the hell are you?"

"You're standing on the brink of something truly amazing, Professor Hale. You are about to be given an opportunity that few men will ever have."

"Where's Stephanie?" Hale snapped.

"There's no need to trouble yourself about Miss Miller. I can promise you that she is in good hands, and that she is safe and sound. She is in no danger, whatsoever."

"What the hell do you want with me?"

"Professor Hale, we've been watching you with a great deal of interest. You're a very intelligent man, and obviously one who is deeply committed to achieving his goals. We admire that."

"You keep saying 'we.' Who are you?"

There was a pause.

"We are a group of individuals who have been given a great responsibility. We would like for you to join our ranks and to do something truly important with your life."

"For someone who wants me to join with them, you might rethink the whole keeping me a prisoner strategy."

There came a dry chuckle. "When the time is right, you'll be given the chance to leave, of course. We just wanted you to hear our proposal before you made any sort of rash decision."

"What in the world makes you think that I'd help you?" Hale asked. "From everything I've seen, you're a bunch of murderers who seem to think that it's perfectly fine to take a person's life."

"If that's what you think about us, you're mistaken. Granted, there were some unpleasant tasks that needed to be done, but there was no choice in the matter. They had to be handled. We are a group of individuals who takes the long-term view about things. It's easy to sit back and make judgment calls when there's nothing on the line. It's something else entirely when you realize that the decisions that have to be made are far-reaching and more important than anyone can ever know."

"And what happens to me if I don't agree to go along with you?" Hale asked. "Do I become another unpleasant task?"

"Professor Hale, let's not get ahead of ourselves here. Let's simply take this one step at a time. Now, for the moment, all we want from you is to be open to any proposal that we might give to you. In return, we will provide you a sign of our good faith."

The door opened, then, and Stephanie walked in.

For a moment, she just stood there, as if afraid that she was in a dream, and then she rushed over to Hale, throwing her arms around him.

"You see, Professor Hale? We can cooperate and work together. The two of you are free to leave. We'll be in touch."

***

When Darley returned to Headquarters, a young uniformed officer informed him that the Chief Superintendent wanted to meet with him immediately.

"Did he say what he wanted?" Darley asked.

The officer shook his head. "No, sir."

Heading towards his superior's office, Darley braced himself for the inevitable chewing out that was going to come from the fact that he wasn't moving fast enough for those above him. There had been serious crimes committed and there were those out there who wanted to see results.

When he reached the office, the attractive blonde receptionist said, "Just go right on in, Inspector. He's expecting you."

Darley opened the door to the inner office and found Chief Superintendent William Auricson sitting there, a tight expression on his heavy-set features. Auricson had been put into place by the political machine, as he was one of those individuals who was quite skilled at following orders and not doing too much thinking on his own.

No one in the department with any sort of backbone had a use for the man.

"Have a seat, Darley," Auricson said. "I was wondering when you were going to show up."

Darley bit back the comment he wanted to make in reply and simply said, "Sorry about that, Superintendent. I was working on the Miller and associated homicides, and I didn't get back to the office until just now."

Auricson shrugged.

"Whatever. Right now, we have more important things to concern ourselves with."

"Sir?" Darley asked, confused.

"There have been allegations made against you, and I'm afraid that they're quite serious."

"What sort of allegations?" Darley asked. "When did this happen?"

"This morning. A prominent individual informed us

that you have been engaging in harassment behavior, and he threatened us with legal action if we did not do something about you. Therefore, pending a full investigation, you are being placed on a temporary leave of absence."

Darley rose to his feet, barely able to keep himself under control.

"This is ridiculous! I'm trying to get to the bottom of a string of murders here and I don't have time for any political nonsense. Who was it who filed the complaint against me?"

Auricson gave him a long look. "It was Edgard Cheever."

Darley exploded. "Sir, with all due respect, Cheever is involved with this mess up to his eyeballs! How can you sit there and even think about giving any credence to what the man is saying?"

Auricson's face tightened. "You will not speak to me in such a manner, Inspector Darley! Edgard Cheever is a friend to this police department and if he makes allegations about someone under me, I am going to investigate it thoroughly. Frankly, given your current attitude right now, I can't say that you're making a very good case for yourself."

Darley clamped his mouth shut on what he wanted to say, and instead, took a deep breath. "I'm sorry, sir. This caught me by surprise."

"I'm sure there's nothing to the allegations and that this whole thing is a simple mix-up, Inspector, but for the moment, my hands are tied. I've got to follow through."

Darley rose stiffly. "Is that all?"

Auricson nodded, turning his attention to a stack of papers.

***

The ride back to the hotel room was mostly silent. Both Hale and Stephanie were lost in their own thoughts. For his part, Hale was just grateful that Stephanie had not been harmed, but there was a look of lingering terror in her eyes that he couldn't escape.

When they entered their room, both of them started talking immediately, and Hale finally said, "Before we get into this, I want to call the university and find out if there have been any messages left for me. I've been out of touch for a little too long."

She nodded. "That's fine. I want to go and freshen up a bit myself."

Stephanie went into the bathroom and Hale waited until she closed the door before he placed his call to the university.

He reached his secretary, Madeline, after a few moments.

The moment that he heard her voice, he knew that something serious was going on. Hale braced himself for more bad news. It was in her tone. "Sorry that I haven't checked in, Madeline, but things have been a little crazy where I am."

There was a pause.

"Things are crazy here, too, Professor Hale."

"How so?"

"You've been placed on academic suspension."

The words hit Hale like a punch in the gut. For a university professor to be placed on academic suspension, someone must have made some serious charges against him.

"Why am I suspended?"

There was another pause.

"There's talk that you kidnapped a female student and that you held her hostage."

For a moment, Hale couldn't understand what he'd heard, and then, he burst into laughter. A wave of relief washed over him.

"If you're talking about Stephanie Miller, I'm sorry to

disappoint you, Madeline, but I definitely didn't kidnap her. She and I have been doing some research into her father's death."

"There were other things, too, Professor Hale."

"Like what?"

"The Dean himself was contacted by someone high up in the French government, and there were things said about you. I don't know all the details, but whoever talked to the Dean made it sound as if you'd lost your mind."

The relief Hale had experienced moments ago was gone. If there were high ranking officials speaking out against him, he had no doubt that the university would do whatever it took to wash its hands of him – which is what they were doing.

Hale remembered a professor from years ago – a man named William Whitecliffe. He had been a well-liked individual, but somewhere along the line, he had run afoul of a couple of other professors, and they had begun a campaign against him.

At first, Whitecliffe hadn't taken the threat seriously, but after it had gone on for a while, he had discovered that people who he'd thought were his friends had turned against him.

And now, Hale wondered if the same thing was going to happen to him.

"Madeline, I want you to know that whatever you hear about me isn't the truth."

"Professor Hale, I've worked for you for five years and I think I've got a good idea as to the kind of man you are. I can smell when someone's being set up and I know that someone's spreading a lot of lies."

A wave of gratitude washed over him.

"Thanks, Madeline."

"I'm supposed to notify the Dean's Office the moment

that you get in touch with me, but as far as I'm concerned, Professor Hale, you never called."

He grinned.

"Thanks, Madeline."

"You need to get to the bottom of things over there, though – that way, you can clear yourself."

"That's what I'm working on," he told her, and hung up.

A few moments later, Stephanie emerged from the bathroom. She had on a hotel bathrobe, and it looked as if she'd washed her face and put on a little makeup.

She sat down next to Hale on the bed.

"How are you feeling?" he asked.

She sighed. "I've been better."

"So have I," he replied, and explained what he'd learned from Madeline.

When he was done, she burst into tears.

For a moment, Hale was caught off-guard and didn't know what to do. Then, he put his arms around her and pulled her close.

He let her cry it out.

When she was done, she pulled away and gave him a long, searching look. Hale saw the truth in that gaze, and he managed a wry smile.

"You're leaving," he said, softly

She nodded. "James, I can't deal with this. I know that I should be avenging my father's death, but I'm frightened. The people who are behind this don't play by any kind of rules – and they have too damned much power. They can do whatever the hell they want and there's no one to stop them."

Hale sighed. "I know – and I'm glad that you're the one who came up with this, because after the conversation with Madeline, I've decided that you need to get back to your life.

There's way too much danger here right now, and I can't afford to try to get to the bottom of things and worry about you, at the same time. Besides, your father would not have wanted you to be placing yourself in danger over him."

She stared at him. "You're still going through with this?" she asked, incredulously.

"I have to. Right now, whoever is behind this has me behind the eight-ball. If I don't get to the bottom of things, I'll have lost my position at the university and I'll have been thrown out into the cold. I need to find out who's behind this so that I can expose them and get my life back."

Stephanie's eyes held his. "You don't hate me for being such a baby?" she asked, softly.

Hale touched her face gently. "In a thousand years, Stephanie, I could never hate you."

***

Hale sat on the edge of the bed in the hotel room, a deck of playing cards that he'd picked up in the gift shop in his hand. He'd removed the four kings and had them set out on the bed, trying to understand just what was going on.

There was a mystery here that he couldn't walk away from, a puzzle that needed to be solved. It wasn't just a question of intellectual curiosity, although that was a part of it. More than that, though, there was the question of making sure that he got to the bottom of what had happened to Aaron Miller.

Stephanie was in the restaurant, and Hale knew that she was embarrassed about leaving him behind while she returned to her life. He'd tried to make her understand that he supported her decision, but it didn't matter. He knew she felt as if she were letting her father down.

Someone knocked on the door.

Hale looked out the security lens and saw Darley

standing there.

Opening the door, Hale let the detective in. One look at the man's face, however, told him that something was seriously wrong.

"What's going on, Darley?"

The police officer shook his head. "I've been placed on leave, pending an investigation into allegations that were made against me," he said, disgusted.

"What allegations?"

Darley shrugged. "The department hasn't seen fit to tell me that much information," he snapped.

"That's the most ridiculous thing I've ever heard of."

"Welcome to the world of politics, professor. That's how things are done. Obviously, I've been getting some people upset – the kind of people who have enough clout to get me pulled from the case. Of course, after things die down, I'll get my job back – on the unspoken condition that I don't stir things up again."

"So, you're supposed to just let someone get away with murder."

Darley nodded.

"That's the general idea."

At that moment, Darley's phone rang, and he walked towards the door to take the call.

Hale gathered the cards together and watched for Darley to finish with his phone call. When the detective was finished, he went over to the television in the room and turned it on.

"That was one of my contacts," Darley explained, "and he told me that if I want to understand what's going on, I need to turn on the news right now. Apparently, something big is going down."

"What is it?" Hale asked.

The screen was filled with what looked like a massive riot taking place – and the words "LIVE COVERAGE" superimposed on the screen.

"What the hell is going on?" Hale asked, stunned.

Darley shook his head.

"The world, my friend, looks like it's going crazy, I suppose."

CHAPTER SEVENTEEN

The President turned away from the riots on his television screen and gave his Vice-President a long, hard look.

"Look at them out there – behaving like animals! What the hell are they thinking?"

The Vice-President shrugged. "A mob doesn't need to think. It just acts."

From the far end of the President's office, General Dumont cleared his throat. Tall, with dark eyes and a sardonic smile on his lips, he appeared to find the entire episode amusing.

Next to him stood Colonel Safir, a pale man with watery eyes.

"What is it, Dumont?" the President asked.

"I think that it's time to deploy the army, Monsieur President."

"Out of the question. The army is the reason these riots are taking place – your damned people have attacking the Albanian refugees like they were common street criminals. I've launched half a dozen investigations into rape allegations brought forward by Albanian women, and the eyewitness reports of what your people have to the Albanian men are horrific."

Dumont shook his head.

"You cannot hold the entire army responsible for what a handful of rogue soldiers have done. We have launched an investigation and when we find those responsible, they will be brought to justice."

The President regarded Dumont in silence for a long moment. "I wonder how many high-ranking officials will be brought forward, General."

Dumont raised one eyebrow. "I'm afraid that I'm not

following you, Monsieur President."

"I've been hearing rumors, General Dumont – whispers that those high up are actively working behind the scenes to cause problems for the government."

The general shook his head.

"I wouldn't listen to idle gossip. You have more important things to worry about."

"I'm not bringing the army into this."

"I don't see what choice you have."

"If I may present an idea," the Vice-President said, his soft voice cutting through the tension between the two men.

They turned to him.

"I think that you have to go public, sir, Monsieur President, and address the nation. It's the only way."

The President shook his head.

"Absolutely not. Right now, I just may be the most hated man in France. Going out among them would only lead to more violence, I'm afraid."

The Vice-President frowned. "You may be right. On the other hand, if you sent me out there to speak on your behalf, it might calm down some of the tension. Granted, there are still going to be those who don't want to listen to reason, but at least it will show that the Administration is taking them seriously and is not simply hoping this entire mess will disappear."

The President closed his eyes, taking a deep breath.

After a moment, he nodded and opened his eyes. "Right now, I think that you might be right. It's not going to end the riots, but it might get some of the protesters to listen to reason," he said, then added, "Who would have thought that the day would come when I'd have to hide behind my Vice-President in order to keep my country from exploding?'

The Vice-President gave him a grim nod. "There is no

other way, I'm afraid."

***

Sitting on the bed next to Stephanie, Hale glanced at the suitcases by the door and felt a sharp pang of regret that she would be leaving. Then he thought about all that she'd been through and realized that the best thing in the world for her was to get to somewhere safe - far from those who had killed her father.

He turned his attention to the television, where the Vice-President was addressing a group of reporters about the current crisis.

"The President would like to express his extreme unhappiness with this situation," he said, sincerity ringing in his voice. "Needless to say, there will be an investigation into how it was possible for a group of refugees to find themselves being assaulted at the hands of those who should have been protecting them, and I will not rest until all of those responsible are brought to justice.

"In the meantime, I am begging all of those who would take to the streets to allow calmer heads to prevail. You can rest assured that I will make certain that justice will be done and that those who have been wronged will be avenged."

Hale shook his head, turning off the television and looked at Stephanie.

"The man knows how to deliver a great speech, but I'm not buying it. There's something going on here that doesn't make sense."

Stephanie gave him a wry smile.

"James, everything doesn't have to be related to what you're doing, you know. It might be time to think about walking away from this."

"I can't do that," he said, firmly. "Whoever is behind this wants me to be mixed up in the whole mess. They're not going to let me walk away from this."

She gave him a long look. "You realize what's going on here, don't you?" she asked.

"Right now, I'm not sure of anything, Stephanie."

"You're being manipulated - the same way that everyone else has been manipulated. They're planning something, and they're going to make sure that you're a part of it."

He sighed. "I don't think that I have any choice in the matter. Whoever is behind this has enough clout to get Darley taken off the case. That requires a tremendous amount of political power."

"The kind of political power that someone like the Vice-President could wield?"

Hale thought about it for a long moment and slowly nodded. "Yes," he finally said, softly, "that's the kind of pressure it would take."

She went over to him, then, and put her arms around him, her eyes holding his. "Listen to me - you see what they can do. You don't stand a chance against them, James. Just come back to the campus with me and we'll force the university to take you back. If they don't, we'll sue the hell out of them. The important thing is that you and I can be free of this."

Hale slowly shook his head. "It's not that easy. Right now, I'm the only person that can actually do something to stop the people who killed your father. If I walk away from this, they win. More importantly, whoever is behind this is up to something that goes much deeper than just some murders. They're up to something dark and dangerous, and if they're not stopped, they're going to be responsible for something disastrous. I can feel it."

Stephanie gave him a resigned look. "There's   nothing

that I say that can get you to change your mind, is there?"

He shook his head. "I'm afraid not."

Stephanie reached up and gently touched his face. "Then, this might be the last night that I see you alive, James," she said, softly, her eyes filling with tears.

He wanted to tell her that he was sure that she was being melodramatic, but the fact was, he was afraid she was right.

***

Hale gets a mysterious phone call

An hour later, after Stephanie was in a taxi heading to the airport to return to her life, Hale lay on his bed, fully dressed, staring up at the ceiling.

Only an idiot would be mixed up in a situation like this. He understood that. There was no way that he was going to be walking away from this alive. Stephanie realized that, and that was why she had left.

He knew she hadn't left because she was afraid for her life -- she'd left because she didn't want to be around when Hale joined the ranks of the dead.

Then again, what the hell was he supposed to do? Should he just have closed his eyes and pretended that he didn't see what was going on in the world around him? Should he just have ignored Aaron's murder and gone back to his books and his teachings?

That wouldn't have accomplished anything. The people who were behind this were people who didn't like loose ends. Sooner or later, they'd have come after him.

Just like he knew that they would eventually go after Stephanie.

If he was honest with himself, he would admit that the true reason that he was going to see this through or die trying was to make sure that the girl that he'd developed such deep feelings for was able to live out the rest of her life without looking over her shoulder in fear.

Just then, his telephone rang.

"Hello?"

There was a pause. The connection was not great, but after a few moments, Hale heard a man's voice ask him,

"Have you gotten any closer to finding out who is behind your current problems, Hale?"

"Who is this?"

A cold laugh reached him. "Let's not be naive. I'm not going to tell you my name, as I've grown rather fond of being able to live."

"What do you want?"

"Have you been following the news?"

"If you're talking about the riots -- yes, I've been following them."

"What do you make of them?"

"What do you mean?" Hale asked. "For Christ's sake, will you people stop playing games with me? Just come right out and tell me whatever it is that you want to tell me. If you can't do that, you might as well just hang up the phone right now."

The caller laughed again. "They told me that you had a lot of spunk, Hale. You want to know who's behind what's going on, you need to focus your attention on Edgard Cheever."

Hale's heart pounded. "Let's say that I believe you and that this isn't some kind of a set-up. What does Cheever have to gain with the riots?"

"Surely you noticed the Vice-President has been doing a great deal of work in order to keep things under control."

Hale nodded. "I've noticed."

"He's positioning himself to take control when the

President is out of the picture."

"What are you talking about?"

"The same people who are behind Cheever and the Vice-President want to make sure that their people are in power. In order to do that, they need to stack the deck in their favor. This has always been about putting their people in charge."

Hale slowly began to see some of the pieces falling into place.

"What about me?" he asked. "Is my being here just an accident or was I a part of it, too?"

There was a pause.

"I'm not sure about that. I've gotten mixed signals -- but if I had to make an educated guess, based on knowing the kind of people that are responsible for what's happening, I'd say that they picked you. If they did, you'd damned sure better be aware that whatever they've got planned for you isn't going to be pleasant."

Before Hale could get any more information, there was a burst of static, and the connection was lost.

***

Back in her apartment, Stephanie found herself staring at the open textbook in front of her. She'd been at it for over three hours, and no matter how hard she tried, she couldn't get herself to focus on the material at hand.

It was hard to get into qualitative linguistics dynamics when Hale was out there, risking his life to bring her father's murderers to justice.

Leaving him had been the hardest thing that she'd ever done, but after she'd been kidnapped and held, she'd had a startling realization.

She was dangerous to him.

As long as she was with him, whoever was behind this

would always be able to use her against him. Her very presence might be what got him killed, and if that happened, she knew that she'd never be able to live with herself.

Much as she hated to admit it, he was far safer without her in the equation.

And yet, not being with him was almost unbearable. There was an attraction there between them. She felt it -- and she knew that Hale felt it, too. But, she also knew that until this whole situation was resolved, the two of them didn't stand a chance. They wouldn't be able to have any kind of life until they were safe.

Stephanie sighed, and closed the book.

There was no point in trying to get anything into her head when the only thoughts she had were of a man whose life was in constant danger.

CHAPTER EIGHTEEN

When Hale found Darley, the police inspector was in a bar down the block from Police Headquarters, sitting in a booth, getting drunk.

Hale slid across the booth from him, and Darley looked at him for a long moment. His eyes were bloodshot, and he looked as if he hadn't shaved in a couple of days.

Hale shook his head. "This is the last thing that I would have expected from you, Darley. Right now, you look like you're the very epitome of being a total loser."

Darley snorted. "We're all losers, Hale. Haven't you noticed that? The only winners out there are the ones in the shadows, pulling our strings. They tell us to jump and we jump. They tell us to turn a blind eye to all the crap that's going down, and that's what we do. If we don't do it, we wind up being taken out of the picture."

Hale glanced around the bar, wanting to make sure that no one was paying them any attention. "There's more going down than you realize."

"I don't care," Darley snorted, shaking his head. "It's not my problem."

Hale's mouth dropped open. "You can't be serious! Darley, you need to -- "

The inspector rose, and there was a dangerous light in his eyes. "I don't need to do a damned thing, Hale!" he shouted. "The only thing that I need to do is mind my own business, and I suggest that you do the same. Don't you get it, you stupid fool? We've lost! They've won! There is nothing that we can do, and the sooner that you accept that, the better off you'll be!"

Hale wanted to argue, but Darley had brought too much attention to them, and he stood up, shaking his head.

"I thought you were better than this, Darley."

Darley snorted. "Welcome to the real world, Professor James Hale. The view's a lot different than the one you had in your ivory tower, isn't it?"

***

Edgard Cheever sat behind his desk, when he experienced a sudden chill and the sensation of being watched. When he looked up from his paperwork, he saw a familiar figure standing in the doorway.

Cheever did not know the tall, brooding man's real name, but among those in the organization, he was called "Charlemagne." The fact that the man was as powerful as he was and could remain out of the public spotlight bore mute testimony to the power that he wielded.

His presence in Cheever's home was not good.

"I wasn't expecting you," Cheever said.

Charlemagne chuckled.

"Of course not. I trust that I didn't catch you at a bad time?" he asked, going over to an ottoman and sitting down. "There are things that we need to discuss."

Cheever didn't like the sound of that. "What things?" he asked.

"For starters, there is the question of Hale."

"If I were to be given the go-ahead, I could just eliminate him and -- "

Charlemagne shook his head, slowly. "Right now, that is not an option. There are some who believe that Hale could prove to be an asset to us. Frankly, I'd just as soon he be removed from the picture, but that is not my decision to make."

"So, what do we do about Hale if there's no clear course of action?"

"We were tapping his telephone and he was contacted by one of our people."

Cheever's eyes widened.

"Who?"

"We're not sure. Whoever it is is high enough in the organization to know sensitive details of what we are doing, and that means that we're going on high alert."

"What was Hale told?"

"He was sent in your direction."

Cheever paled.

"So, what are we going to do? I'm not going to just sit by and -- "

Charlemagne stood.

"You're going to do nothing until you hear from us. If we think that action needs to be taken, we'll take it."

"If Hale gets too close, I'm going to take matters into my own hands," Cheever said, angrily. "I don't know what you people are planning for him, but I don't want to be left holding the bag when things get hot."

"Don't worry. If Hale begins to become too much of a problem, he'll be dealt with. In the meantime, just be aware that you're on his radar."

***

Darley stumbled through his front door, and nearly fell on his face. There was a time when he could handle his alcohol, but like everything else, it seemed as if that was something from another time -- a time when it meant something to be a police officer, when it meant something to be on the side of right.

"Well, well -- here's something that I never thought I'd see...the great Inspector Darley totally shit-faced."

Darley quickly got to his feet as the light in his living room turned on.

A short, squat little man with thinning hair stood there. His blue eyes regarded Darley with amusement and the police officer frowned.

"What are you doing here, Brian?"

"I came to make certain that you're not dead yet, my friend."

"Blind Brian" and Darley had a long history together. The little man was known for having his ear to the ground and it was said that if anything were to be known about illegal activity in the city, Blind Brian was the one to go to.

"I'm fine," Darley said, going over to the couch and collapsing on it. "How did you get into my apartment?"

Blind Brian looked mock-hurt.

"As if I don't know how to use a picklock, Darley."

"What do you want?"

"I want to find out what it is about you that makes you so foolish. I've been hearing things about you -- things that I don't want to believe."

"Like what?"

"Like people saying that you're playing with fire."

"I'm a police officer who just wants to do his job."

The little man sighed. "You need to focus on making sure that you stop upsetting people, Darley. The word on the street is that you've stirred up a real hornet's nest and you're definitely going to wind up getting stung."

Darley reached over and poured a drink from the half-full scotch bottle on his coffee table. He downed it in seconds.

"I've been stung before."

"Not like this. This is the kind of sting that gets a man sent to the morgue."

Darley leaned towards Blind Brian.

"Why are you doing this?"

"Doing what?"

"Why are you sticking your neck out to warn me away from what I'm doing?"

The little man shrugged. "You've done me some favors in the past and I thought I'd try to square things up."

Darley closed his eyes and leaned his head on the cushions. "Consider us square. You can find your way out, right?"

Blind Brian gave him a long, searching look. "Goodbye, Darley."

* * *

Darley's apartment door swung open silently, and the stranger entered quickly. His eyes scanned the surroundings quickly, and when he was satisfied there was no danger, he cautiously advanced.

He knew precisely where to go.

Normally, he wouldn't have taken on an assignment like this, but the people who had approached him had given him few options. If he didn't want to take the assignment, his eight-year-old child would have an accident.

He had to do this.

Moving forward, he approached the living room and paused. The sound of soft snoring reached him, and he cautiously looked into the room.

The man he had been hired to kill was passed out on the couch. There was an empty scotch bottle on the floor, and on the coffee table, a tray of old cheese and some crackers.

The snoring grew louder and the man relaxed.

Darley wouldn't be the first drunk that he'd killed, and he probably wouldn't be the last. One of the benefits of dealing with them was that most of them didn't even wake up when the end came.

He removed the switchblade from his pocket and it opened with a quiet "snick."

Moving quietly, he approached the passed out figure and brought the knife down quickly, heading directly for the throat.

Darley's eyes snapped open and he threw himself to the side, bringing his arm up and grabbing the attacker's hand.

Caught off-guard, the assassin drew backwards, bringing Darley to his feet.

Within seconds, they were engaged in a deadly dance.

It quickly became apparent that Darley wasn't drunk. The assassin had been around long enough to know that he'd been set up.

His handlers weren't going to like this.

As they fought, neither spoke. Talking would take energy, and right now, both men were focusing on survival.

As Darley moved to one side, the man saw his chance and he swept his leg out, catching the police officer off-guard. Darley went down next to the coffee table, and the killer knew he wouldn't have another opportunity to get Darley in a vulnerable position.

Sudden pain shot through his leg and he looked down to find the cheese knife stuck in his leg, just as Darley flung himself off the floor.

Before he could react, Darley was on top of him, and the killer knew that he'd lost -- which only left one course of action.

When the people who had come to him had given him this assignment, they'd given him something else, as well, telling him that if he failed to use it when the time came, his child would die.

The assassin bit down on the false crown in the back of his mouth, releasing a white-hot toxin that raced through his body.

CHAPTER NINETEEN

Blind Brian sat behind his desk in the bar, going over the receipts for the night. Things had been slow lately, but they'd pick up again.

They always did.

A commotion outside his door caught his attention, and he reached into his desk for the automatic that he kept there, but before he could do anything, the door slammed open and Darley walked in.

One look into the detective's eye told him not to do anything stupid.

"Hello, my friend. What can I do for -- ?"

Darley grabbed him by the throat and pulled him across the desk, then flung him to the floor. "Sorry to barge in like this, 'friend,' but I just had a visit from someone that I think you might know."

"Listen to me, Darley, before you do anything stupid, you need to -- "

Darley yanked him to his feet and threw him into a chair.

The police inspector took out his gun and pointed it directly at Brian.

"Do you want to know what happened to me tonight?"

"You're not thinking straight, Darley. You're obviously drunk and -- "

Darley shook his head. "Haven't touched a drop in days."

"When I saw you, you were -- " Blind Brian began, then stopped, as he realized what had happened. "You were acting, weren't you?"

Darley shrugged. "I figured the people who have been watching me would be more likely to do something stupid if they thought I wasn't a threat to them. Looks like I was right."

"What are you saying?"

"I'm saying that you decide to pop into my apartment for the first time in all the years that I've known you, and later that night, someone comes in and tries to kill me. If I was the kind of man who believes in coincidences, I'd say that was the strangest one ever. Then again, I don't believe in coincidences. I think the people who want me out of the way sent you to scout me out and see how much of a threat I was."

Blind Brian stared at him. "You never should have gotten mixed up in this, Darley."

"Too late. I am mixed up in in it - and you're going to tell me what I need to know."

"No, my friend. That's not going to happen."

"Then I'll see to it that you rot behind bars."

Blind Brian shrugged. "That's hardly the threat you might think it is. You see, the people who want you out of the way have the power to hurt those who are close to me. The most that you can do is possibly lock me up, possibly hurt me. What they can do is attack my family, my friends -- and they'll do it."

Darley shook his head. "Who are they?"

"I can't tell you that, naturally."

"What the hell do they want with me?"

"You were never a part of this. It's your professor friend they want."

"Why?"

Blind Brian shrugged. "I don't know. I just know that the word is out that the professor is given 'hands off' status. But, as for you, they're going to keep coming after you."

Darley nodded. "I know."

"What are you going to do?"

Darley's eyes turned cold. "I'm going to find a way to take them down."

CHAPTER TWENTY

The ringing of the phone brought Hale out of a sound slumber, and he reached out from under the covers to answer the call.

"Hello?" he asked, aware of the tiredness in his voice.

"James?"

When he heard Stephanie's voice, Hale immediately sat up, forcing the sleep out of his system, heart pounding. "Stephanie? What's wrong?"

"Nothing. Nothing's wrong. I just wanted to hear your voice."

Hale let out a sigh of relief, and found himself grinning. "I'm afraid that voice you want to hear is going to sound groggy. I haven't been getting much sleep."

"I figured as much," she said, and after a pause, added, "That's kind of why I called."

"What's going on?"

"I feel guilty that you're looking into my father's death and I ran away."

"You didn't run away. You took yourself out of harm's way. There's a difference."

"I still feel like a coward."

"You're safe. That's all that matters. You've done the right thing."

"Then why does it feel so wrong?"

"Believe me, it's much better for you if you stay where you are and let me handle things."

"Are you getting anywhere?"

Hale sighed. "It's hard to say. Sometimes I think that I'm on the right track, and other times, I think that I'm just going to get lost in this mess. Don't worry, though. I'm going to get to the bottom of things."

There was a long pause.

"Maybe you'd be better off if you just left this alone, James. There's nothing you can do for my father. He's gone."

"I can make sure that whoever did this pays for it -- and I can stop whatever it is they're planning," he said. "Whatever it is, it's big."

"James, please be careful."

"I'll be fine," he told her, even though he wasn't quite sure if he was telling the truth about that.

CHAPTER TWENTY-ONE

Sitting in a booth in a restaurant, Hale listened as Darley recounted everything that had gone down recently. He listened intently, not wanting to interrupt his friend.

"So, whoever is behind this definitely has people frightened enough to risk going to prison rather than telling us what's going on."

Darley nodded. "I can't even begin to imagine the kind of power these bastards have. I've been a police officer for over twenty years, and I've never seen anything like this."

Hale sipped his wine and took a bite of warm bread, chewing thoughtfully. "Whoever is behind this is both politically connected and criminally connected," he said.

"Obviously."

"And the question that we have to ask is what these people are hoping to gain. It's some kind of power play, but I can't figure out what they're trying to get – or why they have anything to do with me."

Darley gave him a long look. "I've been thinking about that, and I'm almost positive that it has something to do with your friend's death."

"What makes you think that?"

"His was the first murder and that's what brought you into the mix. If we can figure out what it is that got him killed, we might be able to find out who's behind this."

"Well, I know one place that we can start," Hale said.

Darley gave him a long look. "Edgard Cheever."

"Very good, inspector. Just from the looks of things, he does seem to have his hand in this cookie jar, doesn't he?"

"He does, indeed."

"Just out of curiosity, though, what are you going to do if he tries to put even more pressure on you? After all, he's already gotten you kicked off the case."

Darley's eyes turned cold. "If he puts pressure on me, he'll find out what happens when too much pressure gets applied to the wrong person," he said, softly. "The most dangerous kind of man, James, is the man who has nothing left to lose."

CHAPTER TWENTY-TWO

Hale emerged from taking a hot shower to a call from his cellphone. Grabbing a towel, he quickly dried off and picked up the phone. "Hello?"

There was a pause.

"Professor James Hale?"

"Speaking."

"Forgive my calling you at this hour, but I was only recently informed that you are in possession of a very unique artifact – one that I am willing to pay quite handsomely for."

Hale sat on the edge of the bed in his hotel room.

"Who is this?"

"At this point, names are not important. Let's just say that I'm someone who appreciates historical artifacts that have religious significance and leave it at that."

"You want the Spear," Hale said.

"Yes."

"How did you find out about the Spear?" Hale asked.

"I am connected with people who hear a great many things. When they hear something that they think might interest me, they let me know."

"Have you heard anything about Aaron Miller's murder?"

There was a long pause.

"It depends."

"On what?"

"On whether or not you would be willing to negotiate a deal – the Spear given to me, information about your friend's death given to you."

Hale snorted. "Obviously, someone's told you that I'm an idiot – which is what I'd have to be if I were to buy into the fairy tale that you're selling right now. What in the world makes you think that I'd trust you? For all I know, you're involved with Aaron's death."

"I wasn't involved with the death, but I know the people who were. They are not the sort of people to trifle with, Professor Hale. They are ruthless and they are dangerous. If I give you the information that you want, it will only lead to more problems."

"I'm willing to take that chance," Hale said.

There was another pause.

"If this is to happen, we need to meet. I'm not going to give you the information over the phone without proof that you will be turning the Spear over to me."

"Agreed."

"I will be calling you shortly, Professor Hale. We will make the exchange – and after that, you're on your own."

The connection ended.

Hale sat there for a moment, and then slowly nodded.

He dialed Darley's phone number.

CHAPTER TWENTY-THREE

Darley slid into the booth in the diner, and looked over at Hale, who was sipping a cup of steaming hot coffee. "Okay, whatever you've got for me had better be good, Hale. You and I being seen together in public can't be good for your image. Just ask Cheever."

Hale chuckled. "I'll risk it, inspector. I thought that you might be interested to learn that I received a phone call from someone who wants to get his hands on the Spear – and who is going to be providing me with information about Aaron's death."

Darley snorted. "If you believe that one, Hale, I've got a great little house on the planet Neptune that you're going to love."

"I know that the whole thing is a set-up," he said, "but I also know that I think that I'm getting close to figuring out what the hell is going on."

"What do you mean?"

"I think that I might know who's behind this whole mess."

"I'm listening," Darley said, leaning back in the booth and folding his arms across his chest. "Ready when you are."

"First of all, I think that I've figured out what the playing cards were supposed to mean. Each playing card was designed to lead me in a different direction, based upon what the cards meant historically – one card symbolized King David, one card symbolized Alexander the Great, and one card symbolized Julius Caesar."

Darley shook his head. "This is too complicated for me to follow. You ask me, it sounds like we're dealing with a wild goose chase here."

Hale nodded. "Exactly."

"What are you saying?"

"I'm saying that the deaths are being used to divert

attention from whatever is actually being planned – if it hasn't already been done. Whoever is behind this wants us to spend our time focusing on the cards and what they mean – but the fact is that the only thing they mean is that the more time we spend focusing on them, the less chance we'll have to bring the actual murderer to justice."

"But who are they?"

"Montague gave me the answer when he was in the hospital, but at the time, I didn't put it together. He said that the Illuminati was behind it."

"And who the hell is that?"

Hale shook his head. "No one is really sure. Some people think that the Illuminati are not even real, and others are certain that the Illuminati consist of powerful men and women who are actually behind some of the most important decisions that affect the world, but they lurk in the shadows."

"And what makes you think that the Illuminati is real?"

"The person who called wants the Spear – and that makes me think that the Illuminati is both real…and is behind everything that's going on."

"Why do you say that?" Darley asked, looking confused.

"The Illuminati believes itself to have a kind of divine purpose, from some of the accounts that I've read about them. If they exist, they have some of the most rare and historic artifacts in their possession – and they are always looking to gain more.   The Spear is something that they would definitely want."

"Do you know how insane that sounds?" Darley asked.

Hale nodded. "Believe me, I definitely do – but that doesn't mean that I'm not right. Everything points to the Illuminati being real, and being a part of what's going on here."

"Let's say that you're right, James – let's say that this

mysterious organization is really behind everything that's been going on. What are you going to do about it?"

"I'm going to do whatever it takes to stop them, Darley – and I've got a feeling that you're going to want to help me."

CHAPTER TWENTY-FOUR

Stephanie sat on her bed, looking through a box that had some of her father's belongings in it, doing her best to get through it without breaking down. She'd already broken down several times, and she knew that she had to just push on ahead and just get through it.

That was easier said than done.

As she opened another box that had some of her father's books in it, her doorbell rang, and she jumped to her feet, grateful for the interruption.

Going to the door, she peered out the peephole and saw Gloria Davis standing there. Gloria was her neighbor and fellow student from across the hall, and Stephanie opened the door.

Gloria handed her some envelopes. "Sorry to bother you so late, Steph, but I've been holding onto these and I've been meaning to drop them off, but I just never seem to get around to it. Tonight, I promised myself that I'd give them to you."

Stephanie looked at the envelopes. For the most part, they looked to be junk mail and bills. "Thanks."

"We must have a new mailman or something, because all of the neighbors are getting each other's mail."

Stephanie moved to one side. "You want to come in for a cup of coffee or something?" she asked.

Gloria shook her head. "I've got a biology exam coming up and if I don't study from now until sunrise, I'm never going to pass it."

"I understand," Stephanie said, with a laugh. "Thanks for dropping this off."

"You're welcome."

Stephanie closed the door, and went into the bedroom, mail in hand. She tossed it onto the bed, and was about to head into the kitchen for a cup of coffee when she stopped.

Heart pounding, she picked one of the letters up, and for a moment, she thought that she was going to pass out.

The handwriting on the envelope belonged to her father.

CHAPTER TWENTY-FIVE

Hale entered the small bookstore, allowing his eyes to adjust to the gloom inside. For a moment, he just stood in the doorway, letting the smell of the old books wash over him, and he realized how much he missed this world.

It seemed like an eternity since he had just been a college professor.

Hale approached the back of the bookstore, where he found a slender, balding man hunched over an old volume. There were some small bottles of glue on the desk, and some thin strips of leather.

The man looked up at Hale for a long moment. "I've been hearing some very odd things about you, James."

Hale nodded. "I'll bet you have."

Hale pulled out a chair and sat across from Leonard Ingleman, respected bookseller and a man who had a little bit of knowledge on every subject under the sun.

"I've heard that you're involved in all kinds of nasty things. What the hell is going on with you?"

Hale shook his head. "It's not what I'm doing -- it's what's being done to me."

Ingleman peered at him intently. "One of the things that I've been hearing is that you're messing around with a certain group of people who you'd be well-advised to stay away from."

"Are you talking about the Illuminati?"

Ingleman shook his head. "Of course not. The Illuminati don't exist," he said, and then, after a pause, "However, if they did exist, I certainly wouldn't want to be foolish enough to oppose them."

"I might have no choice in the matter."

"There is always a choice. You could, for example,

give them whatever it is that they want."

"They killed Aaron Miller and they've tried to kill me."

Ingleman sighed. "And is that what brings you here? You thought that you could get some information out of me that will help you?"

"Something like that."

"Unlike you, James, I am not the sort of man who would want to deal with this group that does not exist. I'm afraid that I can't help you."

Hale gave him a long look, and he saw that Ingleman would not budge on this.

Hale nodded, standing. "It was worth a shot. Thanks, Len."

He started to walk away.

"Just because I am not willing to get caught up in your madness, James," Ingleman said, "does not mean that I can't point you in the direction of someone who might help you."

Hale turned. "What are you saying?"

"I have heard of someone who supposedly was involved with the people who are coming after you. He might be able to help you."

"I'd appreciate that."

"I can't make any promises, of course, but I'll see what I can do."

"That's all I ask."

Ingleman sighed. "I still think you're out of your mind, James."

"I'm a history professor, Len -- we're all mad."

***

Sitting on the edge of her bed, Stephanie looked down at the envelope in her hand.

Seeing her father's handwriting there was almost as if she had a connection to him, as if he still lived in some small way.   She was reluctant to break that connection by opening the envelope and finding out what was inside.

She had no choice in the matter, though.

Unable to put it off any longer, she tore open the envelope.

A sheet of paper slid out, along with a small brass key. She stared at the two items in her hand for a long moment, and at that moment, her doorbell rang.

Her heart pounded.

Stephanie slipped the paper and key into her pocket and she cautiously approached her front door.

Peering out through the security viewer, she found two men standing there. One was dressed in a black leather coat, while the man next to him was smaller and resembled a certified public accountant.

Both men wore grim expressions on their faces.

Stephanie raced back into the bedroom, ignoring the knocking on her door.

"Miss Miller? Miss Miller, we'd like a few words with you," came a voice from the other side of the door.

In her bedroom, Stephanie looked around for a hiding place, but nothing came to mind.

Then, she saw the fire escape on the other side of the bedroom window.

Rushing over to the window, she unlatched it, and tried to pull it up.

Unfortunately, the window had been painted over a few times, and it was stuck. From the living room, she heard pounding on the door, and she cried out in frustration, frantically pulling and pushing on the window.

With a tremendous screech, it finally broke free of the crusted paint and rose halfway.

The squeeze was tight, but Stephanie managed to

wiggle through it, just as she felt someone grab her right foot, trying to pull her back into the bedroom.

Turning around on the fire escape, she saw it was the man in the black leather coat, and she lashed out with her left foot, catching him on the side of the head.

He cried out and she managed to get the rest of the way out of the apartment, racing down the fire escape, praying that they were not going to start shooting at her.

***

Sitting in the office of an old friend that had turned a blind eye to what he was doing, Darley looked at the stack of old reports that he'd pulled. He'd yanked everything that had anything to do with Edgard Cheever, because his gut told him that was where the answers were going to be found.

There were a lot of files there, but that was because Cheever was an influential man who occasionally found himself dealing with people on the wrong side of the law.

Darley was getting bleary-eyed and he nearly missed one small report that had fallen to the ground.

Picking it up, he looked more closely at the file.

It was a basic hit-and-run report, involving a young government assistant named Pierre Salinger. Darley vaguely remembered the case -- it was one of the first ones that Fasset had worked on.

The case was open-and-shut, and Fasset had wanted to handle the case. Darley had let him because he was working on a jewel heist.

Looking at the report, though, Darley saw there was an eyewitness to the accident, and when he saw the name, a chill went down his spine.

Edgard Cheever.

Darley had just slipped the folder into his side jacket pocket when the office door opened.

Chief Inspector Auricson entered, glaring at him. "What are you doing here?"

Darley shrugged. "I've been going stir-crazy at home. I had to get out of the house or I'd have lost my mind."

"You're suspended, Darley. You can't be here."

Darley nodded, standing."You're right. I shouldn't have come in."

"What are those papers that you've got?"

"I'm so bored that I've been going through old files from years ago -- back to when I was just starting out."

"Put those files back and go home, Darley. You're not to come here until you've resolved your situation."

"Yes, sir," Darley said, and moved past Auricson, who regarded him with suspicion.

***

Hale stood at the counter, chopping up some green peppers, watching to make sure the onions sautéing didn't cook too quickly. He gave them a quick stir, and was about to add a little more butter to the pan when his phone rang.

"Hello?"

Ingleman's voice came through. "It's Leonard."

"Good to hear from you, Len. Tell me that you've got some good news."

"I've got news for you, but I'm not sure if it's good."

"What do you mean?"

"My friend has agreed to meet with you."

"Terrific!" Hale said, enthusiastically.

"I'm not sure about this, James. As I said, I don't think this is a good idea."

"I've already told you that I don't have any choice in the matter. I'm the one who was dragged into this, and I've got to see it through to the end."

There was a pause.

"It's your funeral, James. My friend will call me back with a meeting place. He wanted me to tell you that it would be a very public place, and that at the first sign of trouble, he would disappear on you," Ingleman said. "You're to come alone. Period."

"I can do that."

"I'll call him and tell him that you agreed to the terms and as soon as he tells me where he wants to meet with you, I'll get back to you."

"I really appreciate this, Len."

"If this thing turns ugly, we'll see how much you appreciate me, then."

CHAPTER TWENTY-SIX

Parking outside the address that had last been filed by Pierre Salinger, Darley paused in front of the brownstone, then cautiously looked around. On the one hand, he was fairly certain that no one had followed him from the station, but with the way that things were going, it was impossible to be totally certain about anything any more.

In the report, it had said that Pierre Salinger had been living with a girl named Margo Allister. A little detective work had shown that Margo still lived in the apartment she'd shared with Salinger, and Darley hoped that she might provide him with some answers.

He entered the building and climbed the stairs to the third floor, locating the apartment quickly.

Darley knocked on the door.

After a few moments, it was opened by an attractive brunette with dark eyes and full lips. She wore a black t-shirt and jeans, showing off a body that was lithe and trim.

"Margo Allister?" Darley asked.   "I'm Detective Frank Darley."

The girl regarded Darley for a long moment with suspicion.   He'd seen that look before, and he understood it -- she'd been betrayed by the police before.

"What do you want?" she asked.

"I want to talk to you about Pierre Salinger."

She went to close the door, but Darley put his foot between the door and the jamb.

"I can understand that you don't want to talk to me," he said, "but I want you to understand that I'm trying to find out what happened to Pierre."

She snorted. "It's amazing at how easily the lies come of your mouths. When Pierre was killed, they told me that there would be a complete investigation and that the truth would come out. Instead, they came up with a pack of lies and told me there was nothing that I could do about it."

Darley nodded. "I know. I know there are people out there who lied to you and I know that you don't have any reason to trust me, but I can only promise you that I'm on your side. The same people who killed Pierre are out there, destroying my life, and the only way that I can stop them is to find out who they are."

She stared at him for a long moment, and slowly shook her head. "I must be out of my mind to trust you," she said, "but I'm going to take a chance on you -- for Pierre's sake."

***

Hale entered the public park where he'd been told to meet his contact, feeling both foolish and frightened. He knew that he wasn't really cut out for the whole espionage thing that he was currently caught up in, but he also knew that he was rapidly growing accustomed to doing whatever it took to keep going.

The park was one of the lesser known ones, and Hale went to the third bench on the right, just as he'd been told to do when Ingleman had called him to set up the meeting.

"Make sure that you go alone, James," Ingleman had stressed. "If the man that you're going to meet thinks that he's walking into a trap, you won't see him -- and you won't get a second chance, either."

"Don't worry," Hale had assured the bookseller. "I'll be alone."

Sitting on the bench, Hale felt slightly foolish -- and exposed. What if he'd been set up in a trap? Right now, someone could be hiding in any of the nearby bushes, aiming a high-powered rifle at him.

Hale shivered slightly.

Out of the corner of his eye, Hale saw someone

approaching, and he waited for the stranger to keep walking past.

Instead, the man sat down next to Hale.

"Keep looking straight ahead."

Hale did as he was told.

"I've been hearing a lot of things about you, Professor Hale," the stranger said. "A lot of people have been noticing you."

"Tell me about it," Hale muttered.

"My name is Lancer, and for a period of time, I was a part of the organization that is currently out there making your life a living hell."

"How could you work for them?" Hale asked. "What were you thinking?"

"It's not as if they revealed themselves at the beginning, Hale. They're cleverer than that. They hook you in through whatever weakness they find, and then, after they have you where they want you, they reveal their true selves -- and by that time, it's too late."

"Why the hell doesn't anyone go to the authorities? They can't have everyone in their pocket, can they?"

Lancer sighed. "We live in a world of laws, Hale -- and they live in a world where they will do anything to protect themselves. There have been those who tried to stand up to them, and in the end, they were always taken down."

"There has to be a way," Hale said. "Maybe if -- "

"THERE IS NO WAY!" Lancer yelled, and then immediately lowered his voice. "Don't you think that I've been trying to find some way to nail them? They told me that if I cooperated with them, they would leave me and my family alone. They said if I tried to stand in their way, they'd kill my wife. I cooperated with them, Hale -- and they killed her, anyway. We're dealing with animals here and if you think that you can beat them, you're out of your mind."

"Why are you here, then?" Hale asked.

Lancer shrugged. "Because I've been hearing things about you -- about how stubborn you are and how you've actually got them a little worried. I figured I'd meet you, tell you what I knew, and let you take it from there."

"I appreciate that."

"Yeah, well, I don't have a whole lot I can give you -- other than to tell you there's a gala at the new Museum of Modern Art. Several of the higher-ups are going to be there. You might want to check it out and see what you can come up with."

"What's the point?" Hale asked. "You said they can't be stopped."

"That doesn't mean that you can't try."

Hale turned to Lancer, looking at a man in his early thirties, with dark hair and eyes that were holding tight to a world of hurt.

"Are they ever going to be stopped?" he asked.

Lancer shrugged.

"I don't know -- but if I had to put money on it, I wouldn't bet on it."

***

Stephanie looked around the motel room she'd rented, and did her best to not think about what kind of people could possibly have paid money to spend time there. The walls had several holes gouged in them, the carpeting was dirty and had disgusting stains, and she didn't even want to imagine what the bedsheets must have looked like.

Taking the key from her pocket, she stared at it for a long moment, trying to think of what her father had been thinking when he sent it to her.

"I wish James were here right now," she muttered,

shaking her head. "He'd know what's going on."

No sooner had the words come out of her mouth when she took out her phone and dialed his number. She told herself that it wasn't because she wanted to hear his voice -- that it was because she needed his advice.

There was no point in mentioning the men who'd broken into her apartment, she decided.

The phone was answered on the third ring.

"Hello?"

At the sound of Hale's voice, Stephanie sank down to sit on the edge of the bed, and she closed her eyes, just wanting to get lost in the moment.

"Hello?" Hale asked. "Who is this?"

"It's me, James," she finally said.

"Stephanie," he whispered, and there was something in the tone of his voice that she'd never heard before. "Are you all right?"

"I'm fine. How are you doing?"

There was a long pause.

"I've been better," he said, "but I've been worse, too. I'm glad that you called."

"Are you?"

"Yes."

She digested that information, wondering what was going on in his life that was having him come out with information that she knew he'd normally keep bottled up inside. Obviously, things were getting tense, if he was being vulnerable.

"One of the reasons I called," she said, remembering the key in her pocket, "is that I got a letter from my father."

There was a pause.

"A letter? What did he say?"

"It was a blank piece of paper, and there was a key

inside of it."

"What kind of key?"

"It's a little brass key, but it doesn't look like it belongs to a house or anything. It's more like something that you'd see with a post office box or something."

"Or like a safe deposit box?" Hale asked.

Stephanie's heart pounded. "Yes," she whispered. "It would be a safe deposit box."

"Stephanie, listen to me - don't do anything until I get there. I've got a couple of things that I need to clear up here, but then, I'm coming back home."

"What are you talking about? You don't need to come back, James. I know that you want to see things through to the end."

"I'm beginning to understand that there's never going to be an end to this. Listen very carefully to me - I want you to get somewhere safe, and wait for me to call you. Don't go home and don't go anywhere that you might normally go."

Stephanie looked around the dingy motel room and nodded.

"I think I can do that."

"I'll call you as soon as things get to where I can get away from here. In the meantime, just remember what I said - don't go home. I'll call you."

CHAPTER TWENTY-SEVEN

Stephanie located the right bank on the fourth try.

After spending the morning going from bank to bank, taking out her key and trying to find a bank that recognized the key, she'd all but decided that she was destined to spend countless hours in her quest, and to her amazement, when she'd shown the bank to the manager of the fourth bank, he'd said, after a moment,

"That looks like one of the keys to our safe deposit boxes."

Her heart raced. "Are you sure?"

"It certainly looks like one of ours," he said. "Of course, the only way to be certain is for you to give me the name of the person who gave you the key."

Stephanie frowned. "I'd rather not."

"In that case, I'm afraid that I can't help you. Our policy is to set up an account with an individual and for them to provide us with a list of individuals who are authorized to access their safe deposit boxes. If you don't have a name, I can't help you."

She stared at the manager. He looked like any other bank manager – middle-aged, somewhat on the balding side, with an air of self-importance about him.

She finally nodded. "Fine. The key was given to me by my father – Aaron Miller."

The manager nodded and went over to a small computer, and he slowly nodded.

"Yes -- we have an account set up by an Aaron Miller."

Stephanie let out the breath that she hadn't realized she'd been holding. "I'd like to see it, if that's possible."

"And you are?"

"I'm Stephanie Miller."

He nodded, and said, "If you don't mind, we do require some form of identification."

She took out her driver's license and showed it to the manager, who studied it for a moment, and then said, "Just follow me, and we'll take care of this."

The bank manager stood by the door, and Stephanie waited. When it seemed as if he wasn't going to leave, she asked, "Is there something that you need?"

He shook his head. "I was just remaining here in case you needed me for anything else."

"I'm fine. If I do need anything, I'll be sure and let you know."

"Very well. I'll be at my desk if you need me."

She waited until he left the room, and then she took her key out. With shaking hand, she inserted it into the safe deposit box lock, and turned the key.

The box opened.

For a moment, she stood there, unable to move. She sensed as if she were on the verge of a cliff and the slightest movement would have her plunging to her death.

Unable to put it off any longer, she looked in the box – and found a small notebook.

It was the kind of black leather notebook that businessmen carried in their jacket pockets. Stephanie reached in and removed it, flipping through the pages, which looked to be filled with names and dates and locations, none of which made any sense to her.

But, she knew that whatever was in the book was important – or else her father never would have sent the key to her.

He knew he was going to die, she realized.

The reason that he'd sent the key to her was because he'd known that he was going to die. The knowledge of that hit her with a powerful force, and she felt sick to her stomach.

Stephanie suddenly felt as if she had to get some fresh air. The room suddenly seemed oppressive, and all she wanted was to get out into the sunshine, out where people were.

She needed to get out of there.

Slipping the notebook into her pocket, she closed the safe deposit box, and picked it up.

Opening the door, she found the bank manager standing there.

"I was just on my way in to see if you were all right," he said, watching her carefully.

She nodded. "I'm done. Thank you very much."

Handing the box to him, Stephanie thanked him for everything and she all but ran out of the bank, wanting to get back into the world.

She stood outside the bank, her breath coming in deep gasps.

Stephanie knew that she had to get the book back to her hotel room so that she could look through it. She'd call James – he'd know what to do, what it meant.

"Miss Miller?"

Turning around, she saw two men standing there. Both of them were well-dressed, well-groomed, but both men had eyes that were dark and rather cold.

She shivered. "I'm afraid you have me confused with someone else," she said, going to move past them. "If you'll excuse me, I just want to – "

The man on the left reached for her, and in doing so, she saw a gun hidden within the confines of his jacket.

"Before this gets ugly, Miss Miller," he said, his voice soft and dangerous, "I suggest that you hand over the contents of the safe deposit box."

"I don't – " she began.

He shook his head. "You really don't want to go any further with that. If there's one thing that I hate, it's being lied to. Now, I was hired to retrieve the contents of the safe deposit box rented by your father. You have two choices ahead of you – the first one being that you can give it to me. The second choice is far less pleasant for you. I can assure you that if you open your mouth to scream, we will kill you on the spot and then we will take what we want."

Staring into his eyes, Stephanie knew the man was telling the truth, and she removed the book from her pocket. "This is all that was in there," she said.

He took it from her without looking at the contents and slipped it into his pocket, telling her, "Now, for your sake, I suggest that you don't tell anyone what transpired here and that if you happened to look in the notebook, I really think it would be best if you forgot anything that you saw. I'm afraid that if you don't follow our instructions, there might be some rather severe consequences."

She watched them walk away, then, and after a few moments, she broke down, crying.

***

Hale thought about everything that Lancer had told him, and even though there was a great deal of information there, he didn't know what to do with it.

On the one hand, he knew that he was on the right track – but he also knew that he didn't have any concrete evidence to use against the people behind this. If he tried to go public with what he knew, he'd come across as just another kook, seeing all kinds of conspiracies where there weren't any. He definitely didn't want to go down that road.

But, what could he do? Every step of the way, the Illuminati had been ahead of him, and there was no reason to assume that the pattern wouldn't continue the same way.

There had to be an angle that he could use, but for the life of him, he couldn't see it.

While he struggled to come up with something that might work, his phone rang, and when he answered it, he heard the voice of the mystery caller who wanted the Spear.

"Hello, Professor Hale."

"What do you want?" Hale asked.

The caller chuckled.

"Why, I'm fairly certain that you know what it is that I want."

"The Spear," Hale said.

"Indeed."

"If I give you the Spear, I'm going to expect something in return."

There was a pause.

"Professor Hale, let's get one thing straight between us -- this is not open for negotiation."

"Then, I have no incentive to give you what you're looking for."

There was a cold laugh.

"The incentive, professor, is that you remain alive."

Hale felt anger rise inside of him, and he took a deep breath. The last thing in the world he needed was to antagonize the caller.

"Just get to the point," he finally said.

"Very well – you'll be contacted very shortly about the Spear. We will tell you where and when to bring it. Naturally, if you do anything foolish, the consequences…well, let's just say that the consequences will be less than pleasant."

The caller hung up.

***

Darley sat across the kitchen table from Margo, who

sipped her coffee, watching him carefully.

He knew better than to try to push her. She had information that was vital to his investigation, but he knew she had to let it come out on her own terms. If he tried to push the matter, she'd simply clam up and that would be the end of it. If there was one thing that he'd learned from working on the force, it was that if you wanted someone to trust you, they had to come to you on their own − if you tried to push it, you'd only wind up pushing them away.

Finally, she sighed, shaking her head. "I still can't believe that I'm trusting you."

"I can understand why you're suspicious," he admitted, "but I can tell you right now, I'm on your side. I want to see that justice is done."

She shook her head. "I don't think that's going to happen."

"You don't know that."

She sighed. "I know that Pierre was a good man and that he was killed. I don't know why, but I do know that the police acted as if they wanted nothing to do with investigating the case. That's the way that it's going to be. I can see that now."

"I think that the same people who killed Pierre are involved in my life, and I'm going to do whatever it takes to stop them. But, before I can do that, I'm going to need information."

"What kind of information?" she asked, narrowing her eyes.

"Do you have any idea what Pierre might have done that led to his death?"

She shook her head. "I don't have a clue. All Pierre did was go over budget reports. I think that he found something in one of them that made him curious, though, because he said that he was going to report it in the morning," Margo said, softly. "He never got the chance, though. He was killed the next day."

"And you don't have the slightest idea what it was that he found out?" Darley asked. "Please – think very carefully. It may be the only chance that we've got to get to the people behind this."

"Believe me, I've been over this a thousand times, and I have no idea what it was that could have gotten him killed."

"What about paperwork? Did he ever bring any paperwork home?"

She let out a sad little laugh. "Are you kidding? Pierre didn't know how <u>not</u> to bring his work home with him."

Darley's heart started racing. "By any chance, do you have any of the papers that he was looking at the night before he died?"

Margo gave him an intent look.

"A few days after Pierre was killed, a couple of men came to see me. They said that they had worked with him and that they wanted to pick up any paperwork that he'd brought home with him. They were a little scary, to be honest."

Darley sighed. "So, you gave them the papers," he said, his hopes dashed.

She shook her head. "No, I didn't. I said that he didn't have any papers from the office, and they left," Margo said, standing up. "I'll go and get them for you."

CHAPTER TWENTY-EIGHT

Sitting in the hotel room, Stephanie debated whether or not she should call Hale and tell him what had happened to her outside the bank.

She didn't want to worry him, but she also knew that he had to be told what had happened. She didn't know what was in the notebook that her father had left her, and now, it looked as if she never would.

Stephanie dialed Hale's number.

"Hello?"

"Hello, James. It's me," she said, softly.

"Stephanie, it's good to hear your voice. I've missed you."

She found her heart racing at his admission.

"Do you?"

There was a pause.

"Yeah. It's funny – I've always kind of enjoyed being the lone scholar, but every now and then, I've found that it's nice to have someone to share things with. How are things with you?"

"I've been better," she admitted.

"What's wrong?" he asked, and she heard the concern in his voice.

"I found the bank where my father's safe deposit box was kept," she admitted.

"I thought that I told you not to do anything until I got back."

"James, I can't just sit around and do nothing. I had to find out what it was that my father wanted me to find."

He sighed. "I should have known better than to assume that you'd do anything sensible," he admitted. "Well, what did you find?"

"It was a leather notebook," she said.

"My god, that's great! Is it Aaron's?"

"I don't know. When I left the bank, two men were waiting for me – and they took it from me."

Hale sighed. "Damn it!" he snapped.

"James, I'm sorry. I should have listened to you."

"It's not your fault. I should have been there with you. I hate that we're not together right now."

Stephanie smiled. "I didn't realize that your feelings were that deep."

"Are you kidding? If anything were to happen to you, I'd feel as if I let your father down. He would have wanted me to make sure that you were safe."

"Oh," she said, her tone turning cool.

"What's wrong?"

"Nothing," she said, softly. "I thought that the reason that you wanted to be with me was because you...well, because you wanted to be with me."

There was a long pause.

"Stephanie, I'm not going to play games with you. Right now, I'm not sure what it is that I can offer you. I'd be lying if I said that I didn't have feelings for you – deep feelings. But, until this whole sordid mess is straightened out, there isn't a damned thing that I can do about it."

"And when is it going to get straightened out, James? When does that happen?"

"I think that it's getting close. I'm waiting on a phone call to get this last thing out of the way, and then, I'm coming home."

"Even if it means having to leave your mystery unsolved?"

He was quiet for a few moments, and when he spoke, she heard the frustration in his voice. "As much as I hate to admit it, there are just going to have to be some things that I'm never going to know the answers to."

***

Going through the papers that Margo had given him, Darley felt as if his eyes were melting.

There had to be at least two dozen file folders loaded with various documents, and Darley didn't have the slightest idea what he was looking for. It would have helped if he had some kind of background in accounting.

As it was, all he could do was just keep going through the papers and hope that something might jump out at him and attract his attention.

Darley got up from the kitchen table and poured himself another cup of coffee. It was going to be a long night, and he needed as much help as he could get.

Darley opened yet another folder, and although he wanted nothing more than to just push everything off to the side and get some sleep, he reminded himself that something in the documents he had in front of him had led to a man's death.

That helped keep him going.

Plus, there was the knowledge that the people who had killed Pierre Salinger were the ones responsible for ruining his life and career, and who were out there right now, planning something that involved James Hale.

Darley sighed, and started going through the documents.

For the most part, they might as well have been written in a foreign language. He kept moving through them, trying to make some sense of what he was looking at, but the truth was that he didn't have a clue.

He was just about to turn over yet another page when he stopped, staring at one of the names on the page.

Edgard Cheever.

Darley went to the file folder and checked out what the

papers were related to. The folder was labeled "Ra Institute Budget Request."

Darley made a few notes about it, and went through the rest of the documents.

By the time he was done, he felt as if he needed to soak his eyes in a cool bath for a couple of days. There had been nothing else in the papers that remotely interested him, but knowing that Edgard Cheever was involved with something called the Ra Institute definitely piqued his interest.

His instincts told him that he was on to something here.

Logically, he knew that the smart thing to do was just pack everything up and forget it. He was fairly certain that if he let it be known that he was going to play by the rules, he might be able to get his life back.

Tempting as that was, however, it was also out of the question.

As much as he loved his job and wanted to get back to it, the fact remained that part of his job was seeing to it that justice was done – and if he allowed himself to be bought off by the very people that he was trying to bring down, he'd just be another part of the problem.

No, the only thing to do was to keep pushing ahead.

At that moment, the phone rang and he answered it. His Caller ID showed that it was James Hale.

"Hello, Hale," he said.

"Hey, inspector. Did I catch you at a bad time?"

"No. I was just going over some paperwork. What can I do for you?"

There was a pause.

"I'm thinking about just walking away from this whole mess," Hale said.

Darley chuckled. "It's funny that you should say that. The same thing was going through my mind."

There was a pause, and when Hale responded, there was surprise in his voice. "And does that mean that you're going to follow through on that?"

"No," Darley said.

"Why not?"

"Because the people who are behind the killings and whatever else is going on need to understand that people will stand up to them. If I just turn my back on whatever's going down, Hale, I might as well just forget about ever doing anything to keep the scum from taking over the world."

"I understand your feelings," Hale said, "but at the same time, I can't just keep going up against them."

Darley sighed. "So, they got to you, then."

"It's not me that I'm worried about," Hale said.

The police inspector pondered that for a moment. "Stephanie."

"If I keep on pressing this, something bad is going to happen to her.   I can't let that happen."

Darley shook his head. "And that's how they're always going to get away with what they're trying – they're going to go after us through the ones that we love."

"What the hell am I supposed to do, then? How the hell can I keep going after them, knowing that they might decide to just go ahead and kill Stephanie?"

"Look, Hale, did it ever occur to you that the only way that Stephanie is ever going to be safe is if you decide to go after these people, once and for all, and to eliminate them as a threat? As long as they're out there, you and I both know that they're going to keep on coming back to you, over and over, getting you to do whatever it is they want you to do."

There was a long pause.

"So, what do you suggest?"

"I think that you and I need to get together. I have some

information that I think you might find interesting."

CHAPTER TWENTY-NINE

Sitting in a booth in a small diner, Hale watched as Darley took out some file folders and slid them over to him.

"What do we have here?" he asked.

Darley shrugged. "I'm not sure. Pierre Salinger was working on these the day before he was killed. His girlfriend thinks that there's something in here that might be related to his death, and I'm beginning to think that she was right."

"Why's that?"

Darley handed a piece of paper to Hale, and pointed out the circled name.

"Edgard Cheever," Hale said, slowly nodding. "It seems as if all roads keep on coming back to Cheever, doesn't it?"

Darley grinned. "Something like that."

"The Ra Institute," Hale said, looking at the document. "For some reason, that's striking a chord with me."

Darley watched him carefully. "What is it?"

"I'm not sure. I think I saw something in the newspaper about it recently. Wait a minute – it's going to be some kind of fundraiser at the Museum of Modern Art," he said, and then, he started getting excited. "And if I'm not mistaken, there are going to be several individuals from the Illuminati at the museum."

Darley stared at him. "How could you possibly know that?"

"I've been in touch with someone who's been giving me a little bit of information on the Illuminati. He doesn't think that there's anything that can be done to stop them, but I think this is his way of doing something to gum up the works, no matter how pointless he thinks it is."

"So, what are you suggesting?"

Hale thought for a moment. "I guess that you and I, inspector, are going to expand our artistic horizons and check out what's new at the Museum of Modern Art."

Darley grinned. "Hale, I like the way that you think."

"Before we do that, though, I've got a meeting that I can't avoid – and one that I have to go to alone."

"What kind of meeting?"

Hale sighed. "You're not going to like this."

"I'm sure that I'm not, but you might as well go ahead and let me have it."

"I'm turning the Spear over to someone from the Illuminati."

Darley's eyes widened. "Are you out of your mind? Why in the world would you do something like that?"

"I want to get back to my life, Darley. I really do. Now, I'm willing to go with you to the Museum to see if anything turns up, but after that, I'm gone. I need to return to the way things were."

The police inspector shook his head. "Even if it means living a life that's a lie?"

"I'm a history professor. I'm not a police officer. If there's one thing that I've learned through the years of following history, it's that the people who try to stand up for what they believe in usually suffer serious consequences. That's not me."

"And what about brining Miller's killers to justice?"

Hale stared at the police officer. "If I keep on going the way that I'm going, someone is going to have to bring my killers to justice, inspector."

Darley thought about it for a moment. "I have an idea about giving them the Spear, though."

Hale shook his head. "I was told to come alone. If I show up with the police, there's no telling what they might do."

"This has nothing to do with my coming along. It's just a suggestion that you might find useful."

"Dealing with what?"

"I think that I might have a way to find out where the Illuminati are located."

Hale stared at him.

"How dangerous will it be?"

"Not at all, if it's done right."

Hale sipped his coffee.

"All right, then – talk to me."

***

Walking quickly down the sidewalk, thinking about what had happened with her father's notebook, Stephanie found herself growing more and more angry.

Whoever had taken that book must have known that she'd gone into the bank and had taken something from her father's safe deposit box.

There was only one person that she could think of that would have been able to pass that information along.

Stephanie entered the bank, and strode over to the desk where the bank manager sat.

He saw her coming, and for a moment, she was certain that there had been a look of concern in his eyes. But, by the time she reached his desk, he was on his feet, hand extended, giving her a professional smile.

"Ah, Miss Miller. What can I do for you?"

"The other day, when I was in here, I left with something that my father had given me."

He nodded.

"Yes, I remember – his notebook, I believe."

She gave him a long look.

"When I left the bank, two men were waiting for me

and they robbed me, taking the notebook."

The manager frowned.

"That's terrible. Did you report it to the police?"

She shook her head. "No. I was a little too stunned to think clearly, unfortunately. However, now that I've been doing some thinking, I realized something."

The bank manager stared at her, and she saw a hint of nervousness in his eyes.

"What's that?"

"You made a call to the two men that were waiting for me. You set me up to be robbed by them."

The manager shook his head. "I'm afraid that I don't have the slightest idea what you're talking about. I can assure you that there's no way possible that I'd have any involvement with men like you're describing."

Stephanie regarded him coldly. "You're lying."

"Miss Miller, I can understand that you might be upset, given what had happened to you, but that does not give you the right to accuse me of – "

"Do you have access to the contents of a safe deposit box?" she asked.

The manager stared at her. "Excuse me?"

"Do you have the ability to open a safe deposit box with only the bank's key?"

He shook his head. "Of course not. We need both keys to open the box."

"So, you're telling me that you've never seen what was inside the safe deposit box?"

"Of course not."

"Yet, when I first came in and I mentioned that I'd been robbed of the contents of my father's safe deposit box, you specifically knew that it was a notebook."

The manager's eyes widened.

"Well – uh – well, obviously, you must have mentioned it first."

She shook her head. "No, I didn't. I'm well aware of what I said to you and what I didn't say to you. The only way that you could have known about the notebook would be if you were in contact with the two men who robbed me. There is no other explanation."

He stared at her. "I think that you'd better leave," he finally said.

Stephanie shook her head. "No. Not until I get some answers."

The manager looked around, as if afraid of being overheard, and then he leaned close to her. Stephanie moved forward so that she could hear him.

"This is not the time nor place," he said. "I can't talk to you right now. Come back tonight after we close. I don't have a lot of information to give you, but what I've got might be useful. That's all that I can tell you right now."

She nodded. "That's all that I ask," she said, heart pounding, knowing that she was getting closer to getting answers now.

***

Emerging from an electronics store with a package under his arm, Hale headed for his meeting with the mystery man from the Illuminati.

Darley had made a phone call to one of the people in the store – a young man with a shock of thick, black hair who had taken the Spear from Hale and told him to wait for a few moments. He returned from a back room with a thick wooden box, the Spear inside of it.

"What the hell is this?" Hale demanded.

"Darley called me and told me that he needed a favor from me. I told him that I'd do it, and I did it. That's all you need to know."

"This box, though – what the hell is it?"

"It's been specially designed for transmitting information, but there's no way that it can be detected. The transmitter has been built right into the box. There's no secret door to get to it. It contains some of the smallest micro-transmitters in the world. It's more state-of-the-art than our government has."

"And how did someone like you get your hands on something like this?"

The electronics clerk laughed.

"Obviously, you haven't talked to Darley. When it comes to electronics, there isn't anything out there that I can't get."

"And you're sure that it can't be detected?"

"I'd stake my life on it."

"Good," Hale said, "because I'm staking my life on it that you're right."

CHAPTER THIRTY

Sitting on the bench in the southern area of the park where the meeting had been set up, Hale couldn't help but feel as if he were a sitting target.

The wooden box lay heavy in his lap and Hale had the sudden urge to call the whole thing off. If the Illuminati discovered that they'd been set up, the consequences would be severe. He didn't care what happened to him, but if anything happened to Stephanie, he'd never forgive himself.

Get hold of yourself, James, he told himself. *If you don't nail these people, you're never going to be free from them – and Stephanie will always be in danger. There's no other way.*

"Hello, Professor Hale," came a familiar voice from some nearby bushes.

Hale stood up, heading for the voice.

"Please," the voice said, "remain where you are. There's no need for you to see me. In fact, it's probably better for you if you don't."

Hale looked closely, but there was no way that he could make out who was talking.

"I brought the item," he said.

"I can see that you have something, but I really have to insist that you open the box and show me the contents, if you don't mind."

Heart pounding, Hale opened the wooden box and held up the small spearhead.

"This is the genuine item, Professor Hale?"

"Yes."

There was a pause.

"You understand, of course, that if it turns out that you're trying to trick us, the consequences will be quite serious."

"This is the Spear," Hale said, firmly.

"Very well. Put it back in the box and leave it there."

Hale did as he was instructed.

"Well, Professor Hale, I believe that our business here is concluded. Wouldn't you say so?"

"Is that it, then?" Hale demanded. "Are we through?"

"We are, indeed. You've done everything that we've asked, and in return, you are free to return to your life. Be aware, though, that there might come a time when we call upon you for a favor. It would be in your best interest to assist us."

Hale felt anger rising inside of him. "You told me that if I did this, that would be the end of it."

The figure in the shadows chuckled softly. "Professor Hale, just go back to your life. Who knows – you might never hear from us again."

In his gut, Hale knew that wasn't the way that things were going to work out.

***

Stephanie lay on the bed in her motel room, watching an old episode of "I Love Lucy" when her phone rang.

Her heart raced when she saw that Hale was calling her.

"James?" she asked, smiling. "How did it go?"

There was a pause.

"I'm not sure," Hale admitted. "On the one hand, I think that I've given them what they wanted and they should be leaving me alone. But, they also left the door open to the possibility that this isn't over."

Stephanie sighed. "James, is it ever going to be over?"

"I wish I knew," Hale said, disgusted.

"When are you coming back?"

"Pretty soon. There are a couple of things that I want to work out with Darley, and then, I'm going to do my best to return to my old life."

Stephanie found herself smiling. "You know, for a history professor, you've turned out to have quite an exciting life."

He snorted. "Trust me – I'd love for it to go back to being dull and boring."

At that moment, there was a knock on Stephanie's door.

"Someone's at the door, James. Do you want to hold on?"

"No. I'll give you a call later."

After she hung up the phone, she went to the door, and looked out the security viewer, where she found two uniformed police officers standing there.

Her heart pounded as she unlocked the door.

"Can I help you?" she asked, her voice shaking.

One of the officers took her firmly by the arm, and said, "We need for you to come with us, Miss Miller. We can't get into it right now, but your life is in danger."

While she struggled to break free from the grip, the second officer injected her in the upper arm.

She fought free, and as she did so, it seemed as if the world were spinning around. "What the hell did you do to -- ?"

Darkness washed over her.

***

Darley opened his apartment door and found Hale standing there, a grim look on his face.

"Come on in, Hale," he said, stepping to one side.

The two men went into the living room. Without asking, Darley went and poured a glass of scotch, handing it to

Hale.

They sat down, and Darley said,

"I've got feelers out, trying to get information on the Ra Institute, but I'm getting nothing. Hopefully, we'll get some answers at the fundraiser."

Hale sighed. "I'm not going."

Darley regarded him with surprise. "But, you told me –
"

"Yeah, I know what I said, but the more that I thought about it, the more I realized that I just want to get on with my life. Darley, you're a cop. You took an oath to serve and protect. I didn't. I'm a goddamned history professor, and the only thing that I want out of life is to just mind my own business, bury my nose in a book or two, and that's it. That's who I am and that's what I want."

The police inspector regarded him for a long moment, and then slowly nodded. "I can't say that I blame you," he finally said. "If I were in your position, I'd probably do the same thing."

"You're not upset?" Hale asked.

Darley snorted. "How can I be upset? You've already done more than most people would have done. Speaking of which, did you deliver the merchandise that I gave you?"

Hale nodded. "The Illuminati took both the Spear and the wooden box. But, I still think that they're going to realize that the box is wired."

"The device isn't going to go active until a specific time," Darley said. "They can scan it from now until Doomsday and it isn't going to show anything."

Hale sighed. "Not that it's going to make any difference, though. Let's be realistic here, Darley – the Illuminati is all over the place. There's no telling how far they stretch out. You'll never be able to take them down."

Darley finished his drink and poured himself another. "I know that. But I also know that I've got to make the attempt. Otherwise, when I look in the mirror and I see the guy looking back at me, I won't be able to face the truth."

"Well, I wish that I could stick around and watch you get squashed like a bug, Darley, but I'm going back to my life."

"They won't leave you alone, you know," Darley pointed out.

Hale nodded. "They might – for a little while."

"And what do you do when they come back after you?"

Hale shrugged. "I'll cross that bridge when I get to it."

CHAPTER THIRTY-ONE

Stephanie opened her eyes, and it felt as if she'd had her head stepped on by an elephant.

It took all her strength to simply sit up, and when she did, the world spun around for a few moments. She was sick to her stomach, and for a moment, she thought that she was going to throw up.

She managed to keep the contents of her stomach down.

"I trust that you're not feeling terribly awful."

Startled, she saw a man standing by the door to the room she was in. He looked to be about fifty or so, and there was a kind of amusement in his dark eyes. He wore an elegant three-piece suit, and he exuded a kind of supreme confidence.

Just looking at him, she found herself despising the man.

"Where the hell am I?" she demanded.

"At the moment, you're a guest in my house – although I'm afraid that I have to restrict your privileges for the time being. However, Miss Miller, I give you my word that if you cooperate with me, you'll be perfectly safe – and you'll be out of here in no time."

Anger rose in her as she remembered the two police officers outside her motel room, and she said, "You had me kidnapped!"

The man nodded. "Indeed, I did. You see, it's important that you be here with me for the time being. Then, in a little while, you'll be released and everything will be fine."

"Who the hell are you?"

"Well, naturally, I'm not going to be foolish enough to give you my real name, but you can call me 'Charlemagne.'"

"I'd rather call the police and have you arrested."

He laughed. "Yes, well, I'm afraid that if the police

showed up, you'd be very disappointed in the way that they wouldn't arrest me. So, let's just get on with things, shall we? Is there anything that I can get you?"

"I suppose a gun is out of the question," she snapped.

He chuckled. "I can't tell you how delightful it is to see someone with a spirit like yours."

"Why the hell can't you people just leave me and James alone?"

Charlemagne regarded her for a long moment."It's funny that you should say that. You see, to tell you the truth, the only person that we actually want is James Hale. We need for him to do something for us. Unfortunately, what we want him to do is something that he'd probably be reluctant to do, which is why we have need of you."

Stephanie narrowed her eyes.

"You're going to use me to blackmail him into doing something wrong, aren't you?"

"I'm afraid so."

"He'll never do it. If what you want him to do is so bad that you need to hold me hostage, he'll never do it."

Charlemagne chuckled. "You underestimate the depth of his feelings for you, I suspect. Believe me, once Hale realizes that we'll kill you if he doesn't do as we ask, he'll come through for us."

"You're wrong."

He stared at her, and all amusement was gone from his eyes. "For your sake, let's hope not."

***

Hale was heading for his car, when a stranger approached him.

"Professor Hale, a moment of your time!"

He paused, watching as the tall man came closer. He looked to be middle-aged, dressed in working man clothes.

But, there was a coldness in his eyes that Hale had come to recognize.

His stomach sank. "Can I help you?"

The man stood in front of him, and said, in a voice that was matter-of-fact, "There's no need for you to get on that plane, Professor Hale. You're actually not going anywhere."

"What the hell are you talking about? I've done everything that you've asked me to do. I'm through with this whole mess."

"I'm afraid that right now, we need for you to remain in town – if only for a little while. Then, after you've done a couple of more things, you'll be free to leave."

Hale felt like lunging at the man, wrapping his hands around the stranger's throat, but he knew that wouldn't accomplish a damned thing – other than to possibly get him arrested. "I need to get back to – "

The man shook his head. "Actually, Miss Miller is currently being entertained by a close friend of mine, so there's really no need for you to rush back to her side."

Hale charged the man, then, but before he could reach him, the man opened his jacket, revealing a holstered revolver.

"Please try to contain yourself, professor. As I said, Miss Miller is perfectly safe – for the moment. I'm sure that if you were to cooperate with us, you'd find that she will stay that way."

Hale had never felt such rage in his life, but he was powerless to do anything, other than to stand there as his entire life was turned upside-down yet again.

"It's almost over, professor," the man said, "I can promise you that much."

"Who the hell are you people and why are you doing this to me?"

The man regarded him for a long moment. "Professor

Hale, you are standing on the edge of a new dawn. You might not understand that yet, but in time, I'm sure that you will. When you understand what it is that we are trying to do, I wouldn't be surprised if you don't find yourself proud of helping us."

Hale shook his head. "Tell you what, sport – don't hold your breath, waiting for that to happen."

***

The French President stared at more of the televised riots on the television, and he shook his head. Turning off the monitor, he looked at the Vice-President, seated across from him.

He thought about the morning situation report that his advisors had given him, and it made him sick to his stomach.

"Things are still nearly out of control," he said.

The Vice-President nodded. "Yes, they are."

"They're blaming me for everything that's going wrong in their lives, and it isn't fair. I've tried to do right by them, but it's almost as if there's an entire network of people working against me. I've heard some of the whispers going around and they're totally absurd."

"Yes, sir – they are," the Vice-President said. "We've been doing everything possible to find out who might be working against you, but we've come up with nothing."

The President gave the Vice-President a long look. "What the hell am I going to do?"

"The only thing that I can think of – and I know that you're going to hate hearing this – is for you to step down. For whatever reason, the people are linking you to everything wrong with their lives, and I really think that the only way that you're going to get things back to normal is to take yourself out of the picture."

The President snorted. "The only way they're get me to

step down is to kill me," he snapped.

The Vice-President gave him a long look. "Let's hope that it doesn't come to that, sir."

CHAPTER THIRTY-TWO

Hale stepped out of the shower just as his cellphone buzzed. He lifted it from the countertop, and saw Stephanie's name on the Caller ID.

"Steph? Is that you?" he asked.

There was a pause.

"It's me, James," she said, her voice a little on the nervous side.

"How are you? They didn't hurt you, did they?"

"No," she said, her voice strengthening. "I don't know what's going on, but I think that you'd better cooperate with them."

Hale sighed. "Believe me, that's precisely what I plan on doing. Do you have any idea where you are?"

There was a pause, and a moment later, Hale heard a man's voice answer.

"Actually, Professor Hale, that's probably not the kind of information that you need right now. All that need concern you is the knowledge if you do as you're told, Miss Miller remains completely safe and secure. You have my word on that."

"Who is this?"

There was another pause.

"Again, that's not information that you need concern yourself with. Right now, the only thing that you need to understand is that if you simply do as you are told, without any problems, you and Miss Miller will be reunited. However, if you make things difficult, I can't be responsible for anything that might happen to you."

"Listen to me," Hale snapped, "I'm growing tired of all these damned threats and – "

He never got the chance to finish.

The line was disconnected.

***

Edgard Cheever sat in the hot tub in his backyard, sipping a glass of cabernet sauvignon. He was doing his best to relax, but that was proving to be more difficult than he'd imagined.

He couldn't help but feel as if things were unraveling around him. When he'd first signed on to work with Charlemagne and the organization, he'd thought that it would prove to be financially and socially beneficial to him.

In the beginning, it had definitely been a good thing for him, but now, things were quickly getting more and more disturbing.

Part of him wanted to just walk away from everything, but he knew that he was in far too deep for that to happen.

At that moment, he saw a familiar figure emerging from within his villa, and his heart started racing.

Charlemagne approached him, a broad smile on his face.

"How are you, Edgard?" he asked.

Cheever took a deep breath, hoping that he didn't look as nervous as he felt.

"I'm fine – just fine."

"Glad to hear it. I was in the neighborhood, and I thought that I'd stop by and make sure that you were doing all right. I've been hearing some rather disturbing things and I thought that I'd prefer to hear about them from you than from second-hand sources."

Cheever raised his eyebrows.

"I'm not following you."

"There are some in the organization who think that you might be getting cold feet, Edgard. They're under the impression that if things were to get rough, you might be inclined to do something foolish – such as try to save yourself by telling others about your circle of friends and acquaintances."

"That's ridiculous! I'd never do that."

Charlemagne looked at him, and he had stopped smiling. "I can't tell you how glad I am to hear that, Edgard. You see, if you were to make such a foolish mistake, the ramifications would be more than I'd like to think about. Suffice to say that anyone that you have ever cared about would be seriously compromised."

Cheever licked his lips, his throat tight. "I'd – I'd never do anything to betray the Illuminati."

Charlemagne gave him a long look. "I'm very glad to hear that, Edgard. It means a lot to me, hearing you say that."

***

Stephanie had to admit that even though she was being held prisoner, she was being treated well. Instead of some kind of cold, impersonal cell, she was being kept in a nicely-furnished bedroom, complete with cable television and an expensive stereo system.

Of course, it didn't change the fact that she was being held against her will, but she knew that she should try to find a little bit of positive in everything that was happening to her.

She was lying on the bed when there was a knock on her door, and it was opened a moment later by a tall, muscular man with dark hair and blue eyes. Stephanie thought that she'd heard one of the other guards call him "Brandon."

She sat upright.

"What do you want?" she asked.

He looked uncomfortable. "Uh – I was going to order some pizza and I wanted to know if you wanted something. I mean, I can cook you something in the kitchen, but I thought that you might like pizza."

She shook her head. "I don't want anything."

"You're going to have to eat," he said. "You're going to be here for at least a couple of days, so you might as well keep your strength up."

She stared at him. "I appreciate your concern," she said, her voice cool.

Brandon sighed. "Look, I'm not happy about having to keep you here, but the least you can do is try to be a little more pleasant," he said.

She stared at him in astonishment. "You're kidding me, right? I'm being held captive here and you're telling me that I should try to be a little nicer?"

"All I'm saying is that you're going to be here for a little while and it's probably a good idea to at least try to be more sociable."

Stephanie shrugged. "I'm not sure about how things are where you come from," she said, "but I've always felt that if someone is holding me hostage, I probably don't want to add them to my Christmas card list."

The guard stared at her for a long moment. "Fine – have it your way."

And with that, he left.

Stephanie realized that she probably could have handled that better, but it was hard to maintain her cool when she was being held captive.

"Stephanie," she said, softly, "that big mouth of yours is going to get you into trouble."

CHAPTER THIRTY-THREE

Hale opened his hotel room door and found Darley standing there, looking pretty much the worse for wear.

He stepped to the side and allowed the police officer to enter.

"I came as soon as I got your message," Darley said. "I can't believe that they didn't let you go back home."

Hale sighed, going over to one of the chairs and sitting down heavily. "I don't know what the hell is going on, but I'm about to lose my mind. The only thing that I want is to just go back to my life, but it seems like that's not going to happen."

Darley shook his head. "I don't understand. You gave them the Spear, didn't you? You don't have anything else that they could possibly want. Why in the world are they still keeping you around?"

Hale shrugged. "I don't have a clue. I've been racking my brains over it, and it just doesn't make sense. If I were them, I'd want to keep me the hell away from them. But, they seem to want me around."

"Well, whatever it is that they have planned, you can bet that it's not going to turn out well for you."

Hale sighed. "Yeah, I've already figured that much out."

Darley shook his head. "I hate this. I can't even help you out until I get back into the department's good graces, and I don't see that happening any time soon. Damn it, Hale, we've got to do something."

"Believe me, Darley, if you've got any kind of an idea, I'm definitely open to it."

The police inspector frowned. "If we only had some clue as to what the whole purpose is behind using you, we'd know what the hell to do. As it stands, we're completely in the dark."

"Well, I know one thing that I won't be doing – I'm not going to be going to the fundraiser. I want to stay by the phone, just in case I hear from Stephanie."

At the mention of Stephanie's name, Darley's features darkened. "Knowing that they're holding her hostage, it's enough to make me want to go to Cheever and beat some answers out of him."

Hale nodded."Believe me, I've thought about that. The only thing stopping me is knowing that Stephanie might be hurt if I lost my temper that way."

Darley put a hand on Hale's shoulder. "I can promise you this much, though – when the time comes, we are going to bring them down. I don't care if it's the last thing that I do, it's going to happen."

Hale looked at the inspector and slowly nodded. "I think you're right about one thing, Darley – it'll probably be the last thing that we ever do."

***

The French President sat behind his massive desk, going over the daily reports of the activities taking place in his country. No matter how he looked at it, things were spiraling out of control, and there didn't seem to be a damned thing that he could do about it.

Years ago, when he'd first wanted to change the world, he had fantasized about the day when he was sitting in this office, knowing that he would be able to put his plans into effect and help hundreds of thousands of people. Instead, he'd discovered that he'd walked into a world where nothing actually got done – and if you tried to get something done, you'd be hated and reviled.

There was a knock at his door, and Monique, his secretary, stuck her head in.

"Sir, the Vice-President is here to see you."

"Send him in."

She nodded. "Yes, sir. Before I do, though, I just wanted to remind you that you've got the fundraiser at the Museum of Modern Art that you're attending."

The President shook his head.

"I'm not up to it. I don't think I'll go."

She arched one eyebrow. "You can't get out of this. You committed to it months ago, and the press is going to be there. If you don't show up, they'll have a field day with this."

He sighed. "My country is falling apart, and I'm supposed to go and raise money," he muttered, shaking his head. "Fine – I'll go, but I'm damned sure not going to stick around."

"Very good. I'll send the Vice-President in."

***

The man known as Charlemagne stood in front of the bay windows overlooking his estate, staring at the box that his assistant had just brought him.

He found his hands shaking.

"Well, Professor Hale," he said, softly, "it would appear that you have exceeded my expectations."

Opening the box, he stared down at the Spear, and it was as if an electric charge were flowing through him.

This was not a part of the original plan, of course, but when Hale had first come into contact with the Spear, Charlemagne had known that he simply had to possess it. It was an artifact of legend, and it was only fitting that one such as himself should hold it as a new age was ushered in.

And it was a new age that was coming.

For too long, the fools that had thought themselves capable of running the world had proven, time and time again, that they lacked both the conviction and the intelligence to do what had to be done in order to ensure the overall survival of all the nations – and especially to ensure the survival of those in power.

Charlemagne shook his head, thinking about the whole notion of democracy. The very idea of entrusting the running of a country into the hands of the masses should have made any intelligent person turn white with fear. Take a look at the average person on the street and think about whether or not you want them to have your future in their hands.

Of course not.

But soon, things would change – and the world would find itself on the brink of an entire new Golden Age. The right people would finally be in charge and they would see to it that only the very best would be rewarded – and the rest would simply have to be content with being allowed to live...unless they tried anything foolish.

It would be wonderful if the entire process could have been bloodless, but no successful revolution could endure if the masses did not understand the consequences of opposing those in power.

Charlemagne stared at the Spear, and he found himself smiling with delight.

Somehow, having this in his possession seemed to impart to him a special place in history. In future ages, his name would be linked to the beginning of a new society, and he would be seen for the visionary that he was.

There was one last thing to do.

CHAPTER THIRTY-FOUR

Hale had just gotten up from the couch to get him and Darley another beer when his phone rang.

A glance at the Caller ID showed that it was from a private number, and he said, "Hello?"

"Professor Hale – how are you?" came the voice that he had come to dread. "I just wanted to call and thank you for the wonderful gift that you presented to me."

Hale's stomach tightened. "The Spear."

"Yes."

"Listen to me – I want this whole thing to end," Hale said, watching as Darley rose from the couch and approached. "I'm tired of the games and I just want to get back to my life."

There was a pause.

"I can understand that, and I'm prepared to offer you the chance to return to that life that you want so desperately," the mystery caller said. "Tell you what – I have one last request for you to fulfill, and when you do that, you will never hear from me again."

Hale shook his head. "You're lying."

"One last thing, Professor Hale – and then, you'll be free of us."

Hale locked eyes with Darley, who regarded him intently.

"What do you want me to do?" he finally asked.

"I want you to meet with me."

***

The Vice-President sat across from the President, and nodded towards the television. Although the sound was muted, the riots were still painful to watch, and he sighed.

The two men saw a troop of police officers attacking a group of rioters, smashing them to the ground, handcuffing them, kicking them, punching them.

"I can't believe this is happening in my country," the President said.

"Events are still out of control, my friend," the Vice-President commented. "Every time that we think that we've got the situation calming down, something comes along and reignites it."

"Tell me something that I don't know."

The Vice-President gave him a long look. "I think that you're going to have to send in the military."

The President shook his head.

"Absolutely not. I am not going to go down in history as the President of France who sent in armed troops against the citizens of France."

Both men watched the screen as a group of rioters overturned an ambulance, the driver scrambling away on his hands and knees.

"This is insanity," the President whispered.

The Vice-President gave him a long look. "We are living in perilous times now and we can't just keep ignoring the truth that's out there. Sooner or later, we're going to have to accept that the only way to reign these animals in is with a firm hand."

"We haven't reached that point yet," the President said, firmly.

"I understand – but it's getting closer, my friend. It's getting much closer."

"I can't believe that I'm even considering this insanity."

"The alternative is to stand by and watch as everything that you've ever wanted and ever loved goes up in flames. These people want blood, and if they don't get it, they're going to tear France apart."

***

After getting off the phone with his mystery caller, Hale told Darley about the conversation.

"He wants to meet with me in a park just outside the city in a couple of hours."

The police inspector shook his head. "You've got to be out of your mind if you intend to go through with a meeting," he said. "You don't know what this lunatic has planned. For crying out loud, he might be setting you up so that he can kill you."

Hale shook his head. "I don't think so. If he wanted me dead, he'd have already had me killed. I think that something else is going on here."

"It doesn't matter. You can't meet with him."

Hale sighed. "I have no choice. As long as they've got Stephanie, they're holding all the cards."

Darley gave him a long look, then turned away. Hale caught something in his gaze that worried him, and he said, "You want to say something to me, don't you, but you don't know how to put it."

The police officer nodded. "Yeah."

"What is it?"

"You need to think about the possibility that Stephanie is already dead, Hale – and that they're setting you up to walk right into a trap."

Hale frowned. "I can't go there right now, Darley. I can't handle that."

"But it's something that you have to face."

Hale exploded "What the hell am I supposed to do, then? Am I supposed to just turn my back on the whole goddamned mess and wait for a bullet to hit me in the back of the head – or, worse yet, wait for a phone call telling me that Stephanie's dead and spending the rest of my life living with the guilt that I was responsible for her death? I've got no choice here."

The pain in Hale's voice made Darley wince, and he slowly shook his head. "I guess that you really don't have any choice right now."

"Precisely."

Darley looked at his watch. "We've only got about half an hour if you're going to make your meeting on time. That's not nearly enough time for me to get anything set up."

"I'm sure that's what he was counting on when he scheduled this meeting."

"You're going to go in there without any backup, Hale – you'll be completely on your own."

Hale shrugged. "So what else is new?"

CHAPTER THIRTY-FIVE

Standing outside the entrance to the park, Hale paused, feeling as if an invisible sniper had his scope trained on the back of his head, ready to blow his brains out at the slightest provocation.

He took a deep breath, however, and passed through the gates.

The caller had told him to go to the far west end of the park, and to wait until contact was made. Hale assumed that whoever had set up the meeting was going to make sure that he had come alone before they actually went over to him and introduced themselves.

It took all his effort to keep his body moving forward. He felt as if he were trapped in a slow-motion dream, and he'd have given anything if he'd been able to wake up.

It was hard for Hale to resist the urge to turn around and get the hell out of there. The only thing that kept him moving forward was the knowledge that Stephanie's life depended upon him doing as he was told.

Unless she's already dead, he thought, and immediately cursed Darley for putting that idea into his head.

As Hale headed to the meeting point, he passed a young couple who were looking at each other as they walked, and they had the unmistakable look of two people in love.

He envied them both what they were feeling – and the fact that they lived in a world where none of the bad things that were out there were bothering them.

Hale continued along the small concrete path, until he found himself in a deserted area. A lone bench was situation beneath an elm, and Hale looked around.

He didn't see anyone.

After a few minutes, he sat down on the bench, took a deep breath, and simply waited.

Five minutes later, an elegantly-dressed older man approached him. The man gave him a broad smile, and extended his hand.

"Professor Hale, it's a pleasure to finally meet you."

Hale remained seated, staring up at the man with undisguised animosity in his gaze. "Who the hell do you think you are?" Hale demanded.

The man chuckled. "Forgive me, but it's rather amusing to see an academic, such as yourself, looking so adamantly angry. It rather ruins the impression so many people have of professors being dull and boring. Then again, in the real world, very little of what we think is real turns out to be accurate."

Hale shook his head. "Just tell me what the hell you want with me."

"Of course. There's no point in drawing this out, is there?" the stranger said, and reached into his pocket.

Hale tensed.

A moment later, the man withdrew a Cartier watch, which he extended to Hale.

"What the hell is this?" Hale demanded.

"It's a watch."

"I can see that. I mean, why the hell are you giving it to me?"

"Because I want you to look presentable when you attend the banquet tonight, of course. Besides, it's also a transmitter."

Hale frowned. "What?"

"The last thing that we want for you to do, Professor Hale, is to get the President of France off alone and ask him one simple question."

"You're out of your mind. Do you have any idea of the security that is going to be around the man?"

The stranger nodded. "Of course. That's why you were chosen for this. You're a famous university professor, and it just so happens that the French President happens to be fascinated with history. Our contacts have already told us that he is well aware of who you are – which means that it will be quite simple for you to go up to him, ask for a minute of his time, and ask him one simple question."

"What is this question?" Hale asked.

"We want you to ask him what he knows of the Illuminati. We'll be monitoring his answer."

"Then what?"

"Then, you walk away and you get back to your life. What could be simpler?"

Hale stared at the man for a long moment. "Why am I having a hard time believing that's all you want me to do?"

"It's a sad statement that people simply don't trust anyone any longer," the man said. "I can promise you – we just want you to get the President of France alone and ask him what he knows about the Illuminati. Nothing more than that."

Hale narrowed his eyes. "And that's it? After that, you'll let me get on with my life?"

"Yes."

Hale sighed. He didn't believe that this would be the end of it, but then again, he didn't have much choice in the matter.

"Fine," he said. "I'll do it."

The stranger gave him a cold smile.

"There was never any doubt about that."

***

The door to Stephanie's room opened, and the guard from earlier stood in the doorway. She sat on the edge of her bed.

"I was just wondering if you wanted something to eat," he said.

Stephanie nodded. "As a matter of fact," she said, "I'm starving. Look, I'm sorry about the way that I acted earlier. I know that I was rude, but I didn't mean to take it out on you. You're just someone doing a job. You're not the guy behind my being here."

He gave her a cautious smile "Thanks. Apology accepted."

"You're Brandon, right?"

He looked surprised. "How'd you know?"

"I thought that I'd heard one of other guards call you 'Brandon.'"

The guard nodded. "Yeah. It's my dad's name."

"Well, I like it – it's good, solid name."

He beamed. "What do you want me to make you? I'm a pretty good cook – all of the guards here tell me that."

She thought for a moment. "You want know what I'd love right now? I'd love a grilled cheese sandwich. I always have a craving for grilled cheese whenever I get stressed out."

Brandon laughed. "Not only do we have grilled cheese stuff, but we've got Velveeta. You want to talk about the best grilled cheese sandwich in the world? Velveeta and Swiss cheese."

"That sounds great."

"Coming right up," he said, and closed the door.

A moment later, Stephanie heard it lock.

She waited for a few moments, then quickly got off the bed, and went over to the window.

Shortly after she'd found herself imprisoned, she'd gone to the window and opened it. There were bars in place – thick and steel – and from what she could see from her window, she was in a small house in what looked to be a farm property. There didn't seem to be any neighbors around, which only made sense – after all, whoever had decided to hold her prisoner wouldn't want anyone around that might be able to notify the authorities.

The third bar, however, she'd noticed had a little bit more "give" than the others. Stephanie had been working on it for a few hours now, and she thought that it was definitely showing signs of weakening, which was what she needed.

When she'd heard Brandon first coming, she'd decided that she needed to make nice to him. The last thing she needed was for him to keep a close eye on her because he didn't like her. It was better to just go along with him and have him try to keep her happy.

And, even though it went against every instinct inside her to be pleasant to a man holding her hostage, Stephanie forced herself to take the long view and to keep on his good side.

She went back working on the bar.
***
Looking at himself in the full-length mirror, Hale decided that he looked presentable enough to attend the banquet without raising any eyebrows.

His phone rang, and he answered it, adjusting his tie. "Hello?"

"You're still going through with this?" Darley asked.

Hale sighed.

"We've been through this before – I don't have any choice in the matter."

"Look, Hale, we're dealing with some really bad people here. You know it and I know it. They're planning something and they're making sure that you're in the middle of it."

"There's also a chance that I'll be able to stop whatever

it is that they're planning."

"Do you really believe that?"

Hale thought for a moment.

"No – but Stephanie's life depends on me doing what I've been told to do."

"You know, if you want, I could go ahead and activate – " Darley began.

Hale cut him off.

"No. Not yet. We need to have more proof than we've got now. If we make a move too soon, we'll have blown our chance."

There was a long pause.

"For God's sake, Hale, be careful."

"I'll do my best, inspector."

CHAPTER THIRTY-SIX

Ear pressed to the door of her room, Stephanie heard Brandon talking to someone – probably one of the other guards.

Time was running out for her. She felt it in her gut. The people who were holding her prisoner weren't about to let her live. She knew that. She was a loose end, and these people had already shown how they felt about loose ends.

She had to get free.

Going back over to the window, she opened it once again, wincing as it made a screeching sound. Heart pounding, she waited.

"I'll just check," she heard Brandon's voice on the other side of the door.

Stephanie barely made it to the bed before the door opened.

"We heard something," Brandon said. "What's going on?"

She shook her head.

"Nothing. I just wanted to get some fresh air in here. The grilled cheese sandwich was great, but it's made me a little sleepy, so I was about to lay down and take a nap."

Brandon gave her a long look. "Do me a favor," he said, "and don't try anything stupid. I'm trusting you and I don't want to think that you're thinking that I'm a fool."

Stephanie tried to look innocent. "I'm not going to do anything stupid," she said, putting a hint of exasperation in her voice. "I just wanted to get some air in here. That's it."

He stared at her for a long moment, and then nodded. "I'm trusting you."

"And I appreciate that."

Brandon left, and Stephanie let out the breath that she'd been holding.

After waiting for a few more moments, she rushed over to the window, grabbing the third bar and pulling with everything she had.

The bottom came out first, followed by the top.

For a moment, she couldn't believe that she'd done it, but she realized that she didn't have time to just stand around and congratulate herself. It was obvious that the guards were getting suspicious, and she had to make sure that she was safely out of there before they decided to come in and do whatever they were going to do to her.

Stephanie stuck her head out between the bars.

She was on the second floor of a two-story farmhouse, and although the ground looked pretty far below her, she knew that it was probably more of an optical illusion.

Pushing her way out, she was half-in and half-out when she got stuck. Stephanie wriggled back and forth, and it seemed as if she had moved a slight distance.

"Hey, what the hell are you doing?"

A hand clamped down on her leg, then, and Stephanie's heart pounded.

It didn't sound like Brandon's voice, which meant that it was one of the other guards – and she had a feeling that they wouldn't treat her as nicely as Brandon would.

Stephanie lashed out with everything she had.

A surge of triumph went through her as she felt her foot connect with something solid, followed by a cry of rage.

At the same time, she pushed forward with her foot, and that provided her with enough momentum to force her way out through the rest of the bars.

Unfortunately, the force she shot out of the window was more powerful than she'd expected, and she didn't have time to prepare herself for dropping to the ground.

She landed heavily on back, knocking the air out of her

lungs.

For a moment, Stephanie just lay there, but she forced herself to get to her feet, knowing that she had to get as far from the farm as possible.

There were woods off to the right, and she knew that was her best chance for survival.

Stephanie raced for the woods, heart pounding.

Behind her, she heard shouts and a few moments later, there were shots fired.

She pressed onwards, waiting for a bullet to smash into her at any moment.

However, she managed to stay moving, without getting shot.

After a few minutes, she had to pause, needing to catch her breath. Her body ached from when she had fallen from the window, but she didn't have time to think about whether or not she'd broken any bones.

All that mattered was that she had to stay alive and find a way to get back to James.

To her left, she heard the sound of voices in the distance and even though she couldn't make out anything they were saying, the tone implied anger.

She decided the best thing to do was keep moving to the right.

Forcing herself onwards, even though it heard to take a deep breath, even though she just wanted to sink to her knees and gather herself, Stephanie continued forward.

"There she is!" came an excited cry behind her.

Adrenaline bursting through her body, she ran even faster – only to discover that she'd emerged from the woods and was now standing on a highway, with a huge eighteen-wheeler bearing down on her!

***

Hale stood outside the Museum of Modern Art, looking at the long line of tuxedoed and gowned individuals walking into the building.

Under other circumstances, he might actually have enjoyed attending a function like this, but given the present conditions, he dreaded going inside.

He glanced around, wondering how many of the people surrounding him were connected with the Illuminati, or if they were all just innocent bystanders.

It was enough to make a man paranoid.

Finally, he moved up the steps, taking out his invitation and presenting it to Security in front of him.

The tall, muscular man barely glanced at him before nodding and stepping to one side.

Inside, Hale found himself caught in the midst of just about every other fundraiser. They all looked alike, and he began to relax, having been through this routine a few times in the past.

As a waiter went past with a tray of drinks, Hale grabbed a glass of champagne.

He didn't drink it, however. It was mainly so that he had something in his hand, so that he looked like he was just there to attend the gathering.

Now, the only thing to do was wait for the phone call to tell him it was time to meet the President of France.

***

Climbing the stairs to the third floor of the old building, Darley knew that if anyone from the department saw him, they would be convinced that he'd lost his mind.

Then again, Darley wasn't sure that he hadn't lost his mind.

When he reached the third floor, he went to the door at the far end of the hall. There was a large inverted cross painted on it in silver paint, and for a moment, he nearly turned around and left.

Instead, he knocked on the door.

Darley waited, hearing the sounds of movement coming from within the apartment. The door remained closed, however.

Then, there was the sound of a lock snicking open and the door swung inwards.

Kreed stood there, giving Darley a long, flat look.

Anton Kreed had a long history with Darley. The man was a notorious underworld gangster, and on more than one occasion, he had run afoul of the police inspector – only to have one of his high-priced lawyers get him out on the street in record time.

Big, bald, and bad, Anton Kreed had been known to beat a man senseless for no reason other than not liking the way someone looked – and Darley found himself wondering if he was about to be added to the list of people that Kreed had pummeled.

Kreed stared at him for a long moment, and then he said, in a voice that was deep and menacing.

"What the hell do you want?"

Darley looked at the criminal figure for a long moment and finally said, "I need a huge favor from you, Kreed."

CHAPTER THIRTY-SEVEN

Sitting next to the large truck driver, Stephanie tried, once again, to get a signal on her cellphone, and finally gave up.

"Forget it," the driver said, flashing her a rueful smile. "We're in a dead zone here for the next four or five miles. The reception's just awful."

She sighed. "I'll call him as soon as we get a signal."

The driver shook his head. "Lady, I don't know what's going on with you, but I'll tell you right now – you need to watch where the hell you're going. When you ran out in front of the truck, I thought for sure that you were a goner."

Stephanie remembered the truck coming at her, remembered being rooted to the spot, and nodded. "You and me both," she admitted. "I didn't think that you were going to stop in time."

He glanced over at her. "You're still not going to tell me who you were running from?"

She shook her head. "Right now, it's probably best if you don't really know anything. There are people out there who have a lot of power, and let's just say that I'm not high on their 'favorite people' list."

He sighed, shaking his head. "What the hell is the world coming to?"

"Damned if I know," Stephanie said, opening her cellphone and trying, once again, to get a signal out.

Nothing.

***

Hale stared at the two men near the French President, since they were both staring at him.

Obviously, they were there for security reasons, and he wondered if he was acting suspicious enough to cause them to target him as a potential threat.

He finally looked away.

The only thing to do was wait for the damned phone call – and hope that he could get back to his life.

Then again, after all that he'd been through, Hale wasn't sure if there was even a chance that he could return to normal. He'd been given a glimpse into a world that he hadn't known existed, and now that he was aware of it, it wouldn't be that easy to just pretend that everything was back to normal.

There were people in the world who were going around manipulating events, moving into positions of power, and the majority of the world didn't even know they existed.

In a way, he felt like the character Neo from "The Matrix." He'd been awakened to the truth, and now that he was, he wasn't sure if he could go back to sleeping.

On the one hand, Hale could attempt to make the President aware that something was being planned, but the truth was that he didn't have any real proof – and as long as Stephanie was a hostage, there was nothing that he could do to endanger her life.

But, Hale wasn't foolish enough to believe that his sole purpose at the function was to ask the President what he knew about the Illuminati. From everything that he'd seen of these people, they never did anything in a straightforward manner – it was always about deception, deceit, and denying accountability.

His phone rang.

For a long moment, Hale didn't answer it. Instead, he had a fleeting fantasy of taking the phone out, throwing it off the balcony, and just running as fast and as far from this gathering as possible.

"Hello?"

"Ah, Professor Hale – it took you a little while to answer. For a moment, I was worried that you were having second thoughts about cooperating with us. I can assure you that that would not be a wise move on your part."

Hale sighed. "Yeah, I know. I'm not stupid."

"No, professor – you are definitely not stupid."

"So, what do you want me to do?"

"It's time for you to approach the President. Tell him that you wish to ask him something, and make sure that the two of you are in private. Also, make sure that both of you stay away from windows."

Hale frowned. "What?"

"Please, Professor Hale – you are so close to finally getting on with your life. This isn't the time to start being difficult. Simply do as you are told, and you'll be fine."

Hale sighed, and glanced over at the President.

"Fine – I'll ask your damned question, and when it's over, that's got to be the end."

There was a pause.

"Trust me, professor – it will definitely be the end."

***

Darley and Kreed looked at the half-dozen men that Kreed had called to his apartment.

To call them "frightening" would be an understatement. These were the lowest of the low, the bottom of the barrel, the literal scum of the earth. Each of them had had their paths cross with Darley at one time or another, and there was no love lost between any of them and the police inspector.

Now, they all watched him carefully, warily.

Kreed looked at Darley and nodded.

The police inspector rose.

"You all know me," he said, "and you know that each

of you has been investigated by me at some point in your lives. What you may not know is that I've maintained a file on each and every one of you, and in those files, there is enough damning evidence to put all of you away for life."

The men looked at each other, and rage flashed in their eyes.

"What the hell is your game, Darley?" snapped Claude Valdento, an armed robber with a long string of convictions behind him.

Darley stared at him. "This is no game. This is a matter of life-and-death. A friend of mine is caught up in something that is going to get him killed if it's not stopped."

Bruno Culruthers laughed. Culruthers was an extortionist and a demolitions expert.

"Sounds like it's your problem – not ours."

Darley turned to him. "You're right. It is my problem – and I'm about to make it your problem, too. Now, we can either do this easy or we can do it hard. Believe me – you'd much rather that we do this easy."

CHAPTER THIRTY-EIGHT

Hale stood in the middle of the library, looking at the President of France, who regarded him with stark curiosity.

"Professor Hale, I have to admit that I've always been an admirer of your work," he said, "but I'm wondering what it is that a history professor has to say to me in private that is so important."

Hale stood there, uncertain what to do. If he went through with what the Illuminati expected of him, there would be far-reaching consequences – of that, he was certain.

He decided to stall for time.

"Monsieur President, I'm sure that you are aware of forces out there that would like to see you taken from power."

The president laughed. "Professor Hale, if that's what you brought me in here to tell me, I could have saved you the trouble. Yes, I am well aware of the people out there who think that the best thing for me to do is step down. I can also save you the trouble of trying to convince me that they're right."

Hale shook his head. "I'm not here to do that, sir. I've watched you in action, and you're a rational, thoughtful man – the kind that we need more of."

The president looked pleased. "Well, thank you for the kind words, professor. They actually mean a lot to me. However, I can't help but imagine that you've got other reasons for wanting to speak with me."

Hale nodded. "Yes, sir, as a matter of fact, I have."

` At that moment, his cell phone rang.

***

Seated behind his desk, staring at the Spear before him, Charlemagne allowed himself a small measure of contentment.

He reached into his pocket and withdrew his cell phone.

Right now, Hale was with the President of France, and

in a few moments, history would change forever.

All he had to do was place a call to Hale's cell phone.

Charlemagne smiled as he thought about how the plan had finally come to fruition. James Hale was going to be the man who ushered in the Golden Age of the Illuminati, but unfortunately, the man would never even know it.

It was all in the timing.

Hale had a Cartier watch on his wrist – a watch that he believed was a transmitter. Nothing could be further from the truth.

It was a receiver – a receiver that was attached to a small amount of a plastic explosive that a team of Illuminati scientists had spent years perfecting.

A fingernail-sized amount of the explosive was enough to take out an entire room.

Charlemagne dialed a number, ushering in a new world.

***

Stephanie stared at the motel television, unable to believe what she was seeing.

After the driver had let her off, she'd checked into a small motel, intending to wait for Hale to get in touch with her. Needing to relax, she'd turned on the television and laid in bed.

Now, she sat up, thinking that she must be having some kind of horrible nightmare.

The reporter stared at the camera, her eyes wide and shocked. When she spoke, her voice shook, and it took her a few moments to get herself under control.

"...repeating the stunning news just in – the President of France has been involved in what some say might have been a terrorist attack while attending a banquet at the Museum of Modern Art. Reports are sketchy, but it appears there was some sort of explosion, and we have our crew on the way to gather more information as we get it.

"As of right now, no groups have claimed responsibility, and there isn't any confirmation as to the full details, but we'll report them as soon as they come in. The Vice-President's office has issued a statement saying that all citizens are advised to remain calm, and that when the time comes, an official briefing will be provided."

The reporter continued, but as far as Stephanie was concerned, the woman might as well have been speaking a foreign language.

The only thing that she knew was that James Hale was dead.

***

The Vice-President stood in the office of the hospital administrator, looking at the pale, worried figure seated behind the desk.

The man looked as if he were on the verge of a nervous breakdown, and the Vice-President didn't blame him. The most powerful man in France was currently under the hospital's care, and if anything happened to him, there would be hell to pay.

The administrator licked his lips nervously.

"Monsieur Vice-President, I can assure you that the hospital is doing everything in our power to make sure that the President survives, but his condition is far worse than we've been allowing the media to know. If I had to make an educated guess, I would suggest that he is probably not going to make it."

The Vice-President shook his head.

"That's not good enough. The entire world is watching France right now. Events that are taking place here are impacting countries far beyond our borders."

"I understand," the administrator said, his voice shaking, "but I need for you to understand that even with the best medical care available, the nature of his injuries is too severe."

The Vice-President frowned. "What about the terrorist responsible?"

"He died from his wounds before we could treat him."

"Do whatever it takes to save the President," the Vice-President said, "and in the meantime, if there's any change in his condition, call me immediately. You can reach me in the Presidential Office. I'll notify my assistant that any calls from you are to be put through immediately."

"Yes, monsieur."

The Vice-President headed out the door, then paused, turning around. "So, in all honesty, are you telling me that there's very little chance that you'll be able to save the President?"

The administrator sighed, shaking his head. "I would tell you that it would take a miracle to save him now – but I do not think that even a miracle could undo what has been done to him."

"That's what I needed to know," the Vice-President said, softly.

CHAPTER THIRTY-NINE

Sitting in his study, Cheever watched on his computer as the news broadcast finished the latest update on the terrorist attack on the President of France.

A feeling of contentment washed over him. At first, he hadn't thought that it could really be coming to pass, but now, as more and more information was coming out, he realized that James Hale was dead and despite any optimistic reports to the contrary, it looked as if the President of France was not going to pull through.

Cheever allowed himself a slight smile.

It had been a long haul to get here, but now that everything was coming together, he couldn't help but experience a feeling that was almost akin to divine bliss. For the first time in his life, he understood what it meant when someone said that they felt touched by Destiny.

Edgard Cheever was touched by Destiny – and he was going to go down in history as one of the men responsible for bringing about much-needed change in the world.

His phone rang.

"Hello?"

Charlemagne's voice came through, confident and strong.

"Hello, Edgard. How are you?"

"I'm fine."

"Well, how does it feel, standing on the brink of history, knowing that you are responsible for ushering in a new age of enlightenment?"

Cheever chuckled. "You read my mind. I was thinking precisely that."

"You see, Edgard? Great minds think alike. Now, what would you do if I told you that I had a little something extra for you?"

"What do you mean?"

"Well, I was going to hold off on giving this to you until a future date, but I'm in a very magnanimous mood right now. I have a surprise for you, and while I won't give it away, I can tell you this much – it involves a priceless Van Gogh that you've had your eye on."

Cheever's heart raced. "I – I don't know what to say."

Charlemagne chuckled. "There's nothing to say – other than you'll meet me and get what you deserve."

"Tell me where and when."

***

The ringing of the telephone woke Darley out of a drunken sleep, and it took him a few moments to gather himself enough to finally locate the phone.

"Hello?" he finally said.

There was a pause, and he recognized the voice as Chief Superintendent Auricson.

"Hello, Inspector Darley. Forgive me if I've woken you," Auricson said, and there was distinct sarcasm in the voice.

"What can I do for you, Chief Superintendent?"

"I just wanted to let you know that there's been some news on the investigation into the allegations against you, and I wanted you to be the first one to hear."

Darley's stomach tightened.

"I suppose that the news you have isn't good."

"It depends upon where you're standing. From where I'm standing, the news is quite good – because it means that a corrupt police inspector is going to be permanently relieved of duty and is probably going to wind up spending the rest of his life behind bars."

"You and I both know that the lies being told against

me are just that."

"From the very beginning, Darley, you've never understood how to work within the system. You've always wanted to go off on your own, handle things your own way, and you've never cared whose toes you've stepped on. Unfortunately, that means that you put yourself into a position to make a lot of enemies – and those enemies have been waiting for this opportunity to watch you go down."

Darley's anger rose. "So, when did you decide that it was more important to play politics instead of making the country safer and instead of doing your job? When did you make the call that politics was more important than doing the right thing?"

There was a long pause.

"Don't be an idiot, Darley. The entire position that I'm in is political, and nothing is going to change that. There's a lot of good that I do, and I wouldn't be able to do it if I wasn't where I was. So, if that means that I have to do things that are occasionally distasteful, that's just the nature of the beast."

"Are you telling me this so that you can feel better about yourself, superintendent?"

"I'm telling you this so that you understand there's a formal announcement coming regarding you, but I wanted to call and personally deliver the news – you are being removed from duty and criminal proceedings are being started against you.   By this time next week, you'll probably be behind bars, Darley."

***

Stephanie sat on the bed, eyes red from crying, and became aware of knocking on the door.

Feeling as if she was moving through water, she made her way to the door and without even looking to see who stood outside, she opened the door.

Darley took one look at her and rushed in, closing the door.

"Stephanie," he said, "you look awful."

She looked at him and it seemed to take a little time for her eyes to focus on him.

"Darley," she finally said, her voice cold, emotionless.

He brought her to the couch, and sat her down. Then, he took a flask from his pocket and unscrewed the top, handing it to her.

She took it and drank, choking it down.

When she finally got herself under control, she handed it back to him and regarded him for a long moment.

"How did you find me?" she finally asked.

He shrugged.

"I still have friends in places," he told her. "I put out a description on you, and the next thing I knew, I found out where you were staying."

She looked at him, and the pain in her eyes was a palpable presence.

"They killed him, Darley."

He nodded, and it took him a few moments before he trusted himself to speak.

"I know."

"They killed him," she said, the anger in her voice, "and they made it seem as if he was some kind of insane terrorist. We've got to tell the truth. We've got to let people know what really happened."

Darley gave her a long look, and she saw the pain in his eyes.

"We can't."

"But – "

He forced her to look at him, and when he spoke, there was an urgency in his voice that made her understand just how important what he was saying was.

"The only chance of survival that we've got is to accept whatever fate they're going to deal out for us and move on with our lives. They're going to take away everything that I am and everything that's ever meant anything to me – duty, honor, decency. But, if I don't deal with it, I'm going to be the victim of an accident at some point in the future…just like you will."

Stephanie shook her head. "It's not fair."

"And if there's one thing that I've learned through the years, it's that life is very seldom fair. All we can do is just try to keep our heads on straight."

Anger flared in her eyes. "James Hale was the most decent man that's ever lived – and you're going to just walk away from that and stick your head in the sand?"

Darley slowly nodded. "I am – because the alternative is to wind up dead."

CHAPTER FORTY

The moment that the Vice-President walked into the hospital administrator's office and saw the look on the man's face, he knew what had happened.

He sank into a chair, and when he spoke, his voice was hushed. "How did it happen?"

The administrator shook his head.

"We're not sure. He went into cardiac arrest at approximately six o'clock this morning, and all attempts to bring him back failed. We had our best people working on him around the clock, but his wounds were simply too extensive."

The Vice-President gave him a long look. "I am sure that you did everything that you could, monsieur, and rest assured that the people of France are grateful for the attempt. Unfortunately, there are times when things simply can't be as we wish, and we have to accept that."

"Thank you, Monsieur Vice-President."

The Vice-President gave him a cold look. "I believe that you meant to say 'Monsieur President.'"

***

Driving down the private road to his meeting with Charlemagne, Cheever felt a wave of satisfaction wash over him like he'd never experienced before.

At long last, everything was coming to fruition, and he was a part of the grandness to come. It was enough to make a man believe in Divine Destiny. After all, his entire life had been comprised of moments where Edgard Cheever knew he was approaching a kind of grandness that would make anyone who had doubted him fall to their knees.

That time had come.

Cheever smiled as he remembered the first time that Charlemagne had approached him, telling him of the glorious secret that was the Illuminati. When he had learned that he was to be inducted into an organization that was out to change the world, Cheever had discovered that deep down inside, he had always known something like that existed.

And now, he was on the verge of standing atop a new world order – one in which men like him were appreciated and where men like Hale and Darley were eliminated without hesitation.

Cheever thought about Darley and stopped smiling.

On the one hand, when the news had reported that Professor James Hale, terrorist, had been killed, Cheever had experienced only one brief moment of regret – and that was that he hadn't been there to witness it.

But Darley was still alive.

Then again, it wasn't actually as if Darley could pose a threat to him. The man was days away from being thrown into jail, and he had been stripped of all his power and position.

It was only right – after the way that he'd treated Cheever.

Turning down a small dirt road, Cheever was a little irritated that Charlemagne had chosen this forsaken location for their meeting, but then again, the man was always one to err on the side of caution.

Cheever spotted Charlemagne's car just ahead and he slowed down.

He came to a complete stop when he saw two men standing with Charlemagne.

Cheever had never seen either of the men before – but he recognized the look on their faces. They were cold faces, the faces of men who were given orders to follow and who never questioned those orders…or failed to do what they were told.

Cheever started to back up the car.

His rear tires caught on something for a second, and

then the car shook.

Glancing out the window, he saw that the tires had somehow gotten caught on a buried metal bar that had bent spikes in it.

Cheever opened his door.

The two men stood where they were.

There was no sign of Charlemagne, and Cheever realized that he'd been set up. There was no Van Gogh.

Only death waited for him here.

Driving to safety was out of the question now, so he flung open his car and rushed into some nearby woods on his left.

If he stayed in the woods and continued in this direction, he knew, he'd make it to the highway, and from there, he could make it back to civilization.

Cheever pushed his way through thick bushes, all the way glancing over his shoulder, making sure that the two men were not right behind him.

If he could make it back to his mansion, he knew that there was enough money and other items there that could get him out of the country. Once he was safely away from the immediate threat, he could work on getting back at the Illuminati, work on making them pay for what they were trying to do to him.

First things first, though – he had to get to his home.

Cheever heard the sound of a truck, then, and realized that he was getting close to the highway.

Moving as quickly and as quietly as he could, he pressed his way forward, all the while looking behind him to make sure that his pursuers were not right there.

Another truck flashed ahead of him, then, and Cheever put on a burst of speed – exploding from the woods, just then.

A wave of relief washed over him, then, and he

frantically signaled for a pickup truck coming towards him.

It was an old pickup, white and filthy, but right then, it was the most beautiful truck in the world.

Before it came to a stop, Cheever rushed over to the passenger side door and flung it open.

"Thank you for – " he began, then stopped, when he saw the driver.

Charlemagne.

Aiming an automatic at him, Charlemagne gave him a broad smile and said,

"You're welcome, Edgard."

Cheever never felt the bullets enter.

***

General Armando Delapreece sat across from the Vice-President, who currently resided behind the President's desk.

"General, we are living in perilous times, and action has to be taken – and taken quickly. The President was murdered by terrorists, and we can only assume that these people are going to strike again. That being the situation, we need to be ready to act. Would you agree?"

General Delapreece nodded. "Of course, sir."

"Now, the terrorist that was killed was an American professor named James Hale. This shows that even the most harmless and mundane of individuals could potentially be an enemy of the state. That being said, I need to emphasize the importance of making sure that you understand that your men are going to have to do everything in their power to make sure that the country does not descend into anarchy."

The general gave him a solemn look. "I understand."

"Good. Now, one of my first acts as Acting President of France is to give the army the authority to do whatever it takes to ensure general safety of the population. This means that your men might be called upon to do something they might find distasteful or reprehensible – such as open fire on a group of French citizens."

Delapreece's eyes widened. "Surely, sir, you don't mean to – "

"I mean precisely what I said. We have no way of knowing how far the terrorists have infiltrated our society, general, and it's possible that they've even managed to work their way into the hearts and minds of ordinary citizens."

"I can understand the need for making sure that the country remains safe, sir, but if we were to attack our own citizens, do you have any idea of what the world community would think?"

The Vice-President nodded. "Believe me, I do – and I give you my assurances that many heads of state from other countries have similar plans in place. Naturally, I'm praying that we never have to actually augment these actions, but I need for you to understand that the time might come when you and your men have to do things that they might find objectionable."

Delapreece nodded. "I – I understand."

"Excellent. Now, there's one other matter that needs to be addressed. We've intercepted several messages from what we believe are terrorist cells to those individuals within our own country who are working against us. I'm going to give these names to your people, and you are going to see to it that they are brought before a special tribunal that I'm convening."

"Yes, sir."

"I also want you to understand that these people are to be considered dangerous, and that if at any time that you or your men feel threatened, you are to take immediate action, without fear of any reprisals. The safety of my army will always be first and foremost – and in the months and years ahead, General Delapreece, you are going to find yourself playing a greater and greater role in the history of this great nation."

"I understand, Monsieur President, and I can promise you that I will not let you down."

"Oh, I'm sure that you won't, general – and rest assured, you are standing on the brink of going down in military history."

CHAPTER FORTY-ONE

The Vice-President sat behind the massive desk, gathering himself for what was to come. In a few short minutes, he would go out in front of the cameras and he would bring about a new world – a world in which the right people would be chosen to run things, and the weak and emotional would be left out in the cold.

The world was a cruel place, and there was no room in it for such things as compassion or tenderness. If a country was comprised of compassionate, tender citizens, it was a country that would be engulfed by a more powerful country.

History had proven this, time after time.

There were others who had opposed the timing of the grand plan, but they were in the minority. The world was spinning out of control. That much was obvious to anyone who had the vision to see the truth. There was no point in pretending that things were going to get better on their own – because that was not about to happen.

The strong had to come in and make sure that control was maintained.

Just then, the door opened and one of the Presidential aides stuck his head inside.

"Five minutes until the press conference, sir."

He nodded. "Thank you."

The aide withdrew, then, and the Vice-President (now Acting President) took a deep breath. He was not nervous, however.

He was simply a man who was aware that he was standing on the brink of history – and he wanted to savor the moment.

The Vice-President stood and smiled.

Time to bring in a new age.

***

The world watched as the Acting President of France stood before the assembly of media reporters and the politicians of France and said,

"First of all, I know that all of us gathered here today are mourning the loss of our president, feeling as if the life of this great man was brutally cut short. However, I want all of you to understand that his death will not go unavenged, that his legacy will not be forgotten.

"He was a mortal man, and he made the mistakes that mortal men make. Looking back on his actions, however, we can understand why he did the things that he did, and we can forgive him any of the minor disappointments he might have evoked in us.

"Now, however, we find ourselves standing on the edge of a dark precipice, and we must either take action or risk falling into the abyss.

"We will not fall!

"The enemies of France conspired to bring about a chance in our country through violence and terror. They used an American professor as their tool, and they sought to bring France to its knees.

"They underestimated us.

"The people of France will do whatever it takes in order to remain secure and safe – and as your new President, I pledge to you that I will see to it that anyone who seeks to bring about an act of terror upon us will suffer the full wrath of myself and the French people.

"We are living in a troubled world, and that means that there might have to be measures taken that are unappealing and troublesome. Rest assured, however, that any measures taken will be with the utmost regard for security and human rights of all people.

"Having said that, however, it has been brought to my

attention that the same forces who sought to take down France with the assassination of our president are still plotting against us. if anything, their failure has made them even more determined to our destruction, and that means that I find myself in the regrettable position of having to put into effect certain regulations that are designed for the overall security of France and her people.

"These measures will include the monitoring of internet traffic, telephone services, and any and all electronic devices that can be used for communication purposes. Naturally, these measures will only be in place for as long as it takes for us to establish French safety, and will immediately be removed when the threat has passed."

The Vice-President paused, taking in the measure of the crowd. For the most part, there was a look of understanding on the faces he saw. Sure, a few looked angry, but most of those gathered were looking at the measures through the eyes of a people who had just had their president killed by a terrorist, blinding them to the obvious truth that was being designed right around them.

"I know that many of you might not like what has to be done," he continued, "and I understand. We are living in a world that has been built on precious freedoms, but when forces conspire to take those freedoms away, we must do everything in our power to stop them – and we will.

"Therefore, effective immediately, all electronic communications will be monitored by a specially trained counterterrorism agency to be established at a future date. This agency will record and analyze all communications and decide whether or not to proceed with investigations and/or prosecutions."

There was a murmur going through the crowd, and the Acting President knew that was to be expected. Whenever citizens found themselves under government scrutiny, they tended to get nervous, but by the time any of them were able to muster enough clout to oppose him, they would have already been taken care of.

And then, suddenly, he realized that the crowd was facing away from him – watching two figures approach the podium.

A cold chill went through him.

For a long moment, he stood rooted to the spot, staring in disbelief at the two men coming towards him. There was no way he could be seeing what he saw, but the evidence was in front of him, and he understood, in a flash of insight, that he'd vastly underestimated his opponents.

Flashes filled the air as the President of France came towards the podium, with Professor James Hale at his side.

CHAPTER FORTY-TWO

The three people gathered in a private booth in Chez La Terre spoke in hushed tones, sharing a good meal and an even better bottle of wine.

Professor James Hale poured some more wine into his glass, and sighed. "I can't tell you how great this is. Knowing that this nightmare is over does wonders for my appetite."

Stephanie looked at him and shook her head. "Oh, no, you don't. You're trying to get drunk so that you don't tell me what happened, and I'm not going to let that happen."

Darley chuckled. "It seems to me as if your student has your number, James."

Hale sighed. "Fine – but I'm telling you, right now, that it's pretty boring stuff. What do you want to know?"

"For starters, how come you didn't blow up?"

Hale laughed. "That's an easy one. When the Illuminati sent me to that fundraiser, it was obvious that I was being set up for something. I couldn't figure out what it was, and I definitely didn't believe for a minute that my job was to get the president to say something on a hidden microphone. We're talking the Illuminati here. There were a thousand other ways they could have gotten the information that they were looking for.

"So, that meant there was another reason they wanted me to get close to him – and after eliminating just about every other concept, the only thing that made sense was that they wanted the two of us together so that they could kill us."

Stephanie stared at him. "You knew they were planning this?"

"I had an idea," he admitted.

"Why in the world would you even have gone to that fundraiser, then? If you knew that something bad was going to happen, why wouldn't you have run as far away in the other direction as possible?"

Hale shrugged. "Because, at the time, the Illuminati had you. I knew that if I didn't go through with the meeting, they would kill you."

She stared at him. "Wait a minute – let me just make sure that I'm following you here. You're telling me that you were going to blow up the French president and yourself in order to make sure that I wasn't killed?"

"Something like that," he admitted.

Stephanie stared at him for a long moment. "James Hale, you have got to be the most incredible man that's ever lived."

He blushed and Darley chuckled.

"Anyway," he continued, "I wasn't planning on blowing up the President – only myself. But then, you called me on your phone, and that's when I took off my watch and threw it into the corner of the room. Then, I tackled the president, and the rest is history."

Darley laughed. "I'd have loved to have seen the expression on the president's face when you brought him to the ground."

Hale grinned. "At first, he looked pretty upset – right up until the bomb went off, taking out half the wall."

Stephanie frowned.

"So, how did you manage to fake your death?"

"Right after the explosion, the President and I were able to literally escape in the confusion. Then, he contacted a couple of men that he knew he could trust, and we set up an entire false premise. We made sure that the hospital where he was being kept knew that if the truth got out, they would suffer the consequences, and we stayed hidden until now."

"Of course," Darley said, "it's where they stayed

hidden that's really entertaining."

Stephanie frowned. "What do you mean?"

"Well, since we had to be somewhere that the Illuminati could never find us, assuming they ever learned the truth, Darley arranged for us to spend some time with a dozen of the worst criminals you could ever imagine."

Darley laughed. "I had to call in every favor I had in order to get them underground like that. Oddly enough, once the criminals found out they would be protecting the president of France, they were more than happy to oblige."

Hale chuckled. "Believe me, the president made more friends than you can imagine. Twelve of the most hardened criminals are now going to have a story for the ages – telling everyone in history about the time that they were hiding out with the president."

"But why did you wait so long? Why didn't you just announce the assassination attempt had failed and go from there?"

Hale shook his head. "We needed to find out what the plan was – and who was involved. When the Vice-President contacted General Delapreece, the pieces began to fall into place."

She shook her head. "You lost me."

"The plan was for the Illuminati to set up shop in France. That would be their base of operations. From there, they'd be able to expand outwards, slowly gaining power throughout the rest of Europe. Once they were established in Europe, they'd move into Asia – eventually having the entire world within their power."

Darley shook his head. "It's scary, when you think about how close they came to succeeding. In fact, everything would have worked out, James, if you hadn't gummed everything up."

Stephanie looked at Hale. "What about the murders?"

"They were designed to lure me in – and to keep open lots of possibilities for blame, later on. After the president was assassinated, there would be all kinds of speculation as to the group responsible. The Vice-President would be able to use the murders as a means of explaining why the tougher security crackdowns had to be put into place," he said.

"So, why did my father die?" she asked.

He sighed. "He was a loose end that no one wanted to deal with."

Her eyes filled with tears. "It seems so pointless."

Darley spoke. "Aaron Miller was the kind of man to inspire a deep friendship in a man like James Hale. If it hadn't been for his death, the Illuminati would have succeeded – and we'd be living in a much more different world."

She thought about that for a moment, then nodded. "I guess you're right."

"I am."

"So, is this over, then? Is the Illuminati through?"

Hale and Darley exchanged looks. "Probably not. The Vice-President didn't give up much information, but he did tell us that all we've managed to do is prolong the inevitable. He implied that there are other plans in effect."

Stephanie gave Hale a searching look. "What are you going to do?"

He held up his hands and laughed. "Don't look at me – I've had more than enough excitement to last me a lifetime. I don't know what's going to happen, but whatever it is, it's going to be someone else's problem. I'm definitely not getting involved."

EPILOGUE

Charlemagne looked at those gathered in the conference room, and he saw the concern on their faces, buried in their eyes.

It was time for being strong and for not showing the slightest sign of weakness.

"I know that many of you are wondering what the future holds for us, and I can only tell you that nothing which happened in recent days was unexpected. In fact, things went perfectly according to plan, and we're quite pleased."

He saw skepticism on the faces before him.

"I realize that it might seem as if this is a setback for us, but in fact, nothing is further from the truth. We always intended for this phase of the mission to fail – in fact, we designed it so that it couldn't help but fail."

One of the American representatives, a short, pale man, shook his head. "That's ridiculous. Why the hell would we want to do something like that?"

Charlemagne smiled. "Because one of the best ways for you to get to your enemy is to make your enemy believe that he's dealt you a crippling blow – when, in reality, he's dealt you nothing more than a slight paper cut. Those who seek to oppose us are assuming that we've been weakened, and that's precisely what we want for them to believe."

"What about Hale?" the representative from China asked. "What are we going to do with him?"

Charlemagne chuckled. "Right now, we're not going to do anything to Professor James Hale. He has acted precisely the way that we wished for him to act. But, when the time comes for the most important step of the plan to go into effect,, that is when he will truly prove useful to us."

"What do you mean?" the Italian rep asked.

Charlemagne's gaze turned hard. "I mean, when the

entire world is under the thumb of the Illuminati, Professor James Hale is going to be the one who placed it there."

The representative from Greece cleared his throat. "I think that you're handling this wrong. James Hale might have been someone that you think that you're using, but in the past, he's proven to be quite resourceful. If you think that you can control him, you're wrong."

Charlemagne nodded. "Oh, we are well aware of Professor Hale's resourcefulness and we're not taking him for granted. Rest assured, my friends – there is no way that James Hale can do anything that we don't want him to do."

They all looked at him for a moment, and the American representative said, "So, what's the next step, then?"

Charlemagne gave him a cold smile. "Professor James Hale is going to kill the President of the United States."

THE END

Made in the USA
Middletown, DE
12 November 2021